"In Drifter on the Texas Trail, author Mark Edwards takes the reader on an unforgettable odyssey from Dallas to Fort Worth and beyond... down Texas backroads and forgotten trails. Along the way you meet a cast of eccentric characters, fossil hunters, and traders – none of whom are quite what they seem to be."

-Brendan McNally, Author: *Germania*

D0465255

DRIFTER ON THE TEXAS TRAIL

MARK J. EDWARDS

This novel's story and characters are fictitious. Any resemblance to actual persons living or dead is entirely coincidental. Certain long-standing institutions, agencies, and public offices are mentioned, but the characters involved are wholly imaginary.

Printed in the United States of America
First Printing, September 2020

ISBN: 9798685492012

Contact Mark J. Edwards:
drifteronthetexastrail@gmail.com

Book Design: Josh Edwards
Illustrator: William Bubba Flint

ACKNOWLEDGMENTS

There were many people that were helpful as I wrote this book. I'd like to especially thank the following:

Brendan McNally, my mentor, who sparked the idea of this book in 2003. **David Sabine**, long-time friend who tediously edited major portions of the book. **Tim Edwards**, my brother, whose big heart nurtured the creation of the story. **Josh Edwards**, my nephew, who took on the laborious task of piecing together all the technical aspects of the book for publication. **William Bubba Flint**, talented Dallas-Fort Worth illustrator who created the book cover and inside illustrations.

And to my long-time partner and best friend **Jan**, who supported my project from beginning to end.

PART ONE

MOTEL 1962

CHAPTER 1

Rain beat down on the hood of the1962 Chevy Belaire Station Wagon, his bedroom for the night. Created of necessity, it wasn't too bad. Just drafty and cold during the early spring days in North Texas.

Salvador and his mother's new boyfriend Zack had another argument. This one almost came to blows.

His mom was a woman of character in many ways. Hard working, respectful, honest. Disciplined with money. Taught Sal to pay cash for what he wanted or do without.

But her weakness was men. Specifically, judging men.

She seemed to gravitate toward those who were initially charming, but deceptive. Not to men who were career oriented or committed to a relationship with one woman.

In short, she picked losers.

When he was in the 9th grade Sal made a decision. If his mom brought home an asshole, he'd be an asshole. Let the chips fall. He decided he was not going to take shit off anybody.

His 'take-no-shit' attitude spilled over into school. Many fights ensued and his mom became concerned. That's when he started sleeping in the '62. To get away from adult bullshit. He got to where he hated any man she brought around.

In the past few months he decided he had to get away. Soon.

****

"Sal, go take the trash out for your mom", commanded Zack as he took a long drag of his cigarette and leaned back in the kitchen chair.

"I always take it out in the mornings before I go to school," replied Sal. He tried to ignore the rude tone of Zack's directive.

"Well," Zack said, "when I tell you to take out the trash, how 'bout you DO it." Zack took a swig of beer and eyeballed Sal with contempt.

Sal's mom looked at her new boyfriend, nervous and confused, but said nothing. She knew what was coming next.

"How 'bout you KISS my ass!" Sal stared defiantly at the man at the table. He felt a raging anger rising inside his body.

Zack jumped up from the table and headed toward Sal. He was furious. He hated teenagers with an attitude.

Sal eased up from the living room chair and walked slowly toward Zack, fist tight and eyes on fire.

"SAL!!", his mom yelled. "Control your temper! You get angry too easily. You can take out the trash in the morning." She was frightened.

Sal was about to explode and unload on this idiot. But he knew there was a dangerous energy deep inside. Almost uncontrollable when provoked. His counselor at school had talked to him about it. His friends had said he over-reacted when challenged. Even a girl he liked, Samantha, discussed it with him.

Stop...breathe deeply...walk away, his high school counselor had told him. He knew he had to try to get control.

Shaking with rage, Sal stopped, breathed deeply, and at the last minute angled away from Zack toward his bedroom. He picked out a change of clothes for school, grabbed his backpack, a pillow and a blanket, and walked out of the trailer.

****

It was cold when he opened his eyes. He looked around to get his bearings and began to remember what happened the night before.

An argument. Seething anger. But he had walked away this time. Seventeen-year-old Salvador pulled his six-foot frame up from the backseat of the broken-down vehicle and peeked out into the darkness of their backyard.

He stepped down into the cold wet grass and walked over to a giant oak tree. Looking around to make sure there was no one watching, he relieved himself with the facilities that nature had provided, gazing up at the early morning sky and the rising constellation Scorpio. Must be about five a.m.

His mind always drifted when he looked up at the sky, and it drifted now. He dreamed of travel and wide-open spaces, and to the day when he would leave this place he called home.

Trapped in a world he did not create, he felt a burning desire to strike out on his own.

Freedom. That's what he longed for. A place where he could go and allow his mind to follow his fascinations. And learn something meaningful, not the boring shit in school.

He wanted to jump on a bus and ride. Get in a car and drift out into the world.

He was tired of the constant procession of idiots his mom *fell in love* with, and her *fictional stories about his real father.* He was tired of listening to adults…tired of their lies, their bullshit.

But graduation was only two months away, if he could make it that long. Everyone he respected told him to hold on for just a little longer. Everyone told him to wait. Don't be another statistic. Another Hispanic male drop-out.

But wait for what? A high school diploma? What was that worth? It would get him into college.

And then what? More years of sitting in a desk at school, being bored? Listening to adults, many of whom he did not respect? Getting deeply in debt for four or five years? And then another frick'n diploma?

The more he thought about it, leaving sounded great. Even smart. *Should he leave tonight?*

CHAPTER 2

Peshlakai stoked the flames of the small fire. It took hold and burned brightly in the early morning hours on the high Colorado Plateau.

Smoke. Wood smoke. A scent that brought him comfort. A smell that took him back to as far as he could remember. An ancient smell, one that his ancestors no doubt had enjoyed through generations of the Navajo people.

Burning the fire in the hogan his great-grandfather had built was one tradition he had held on to, one that connected him to the earth, his past, his people. It gave him the feeling of being alive.

He lingered by the fire, hesitant to leave the moment. But knowing that life is motion he got to his feet and put out the flames. Slowly, methodically. A ritual of sorts, with spiritual meaning in each movement.

The day was about to unfold, and an uncertain journey. One he was reluctant to begin.

Peshlakai had received a phone call yesterday from his niece in Texas. His oldest sister had died, and he was listed as the executor of her estate. He would make the trip to Palestine, Texas and take care of the legalities. He would leave tomorrow.

Peshlakai was a physically strong man, even at the age of 76. His health was good, his mind clear, his body muscular, and his path sure. He had always been a man to make up his mind and act decisively.

But on this day, he moved neither swiftly nor with purpose. His heart was heavy from the news of his sister's passing, for they had always had a close bond. Childhood memories danced briefly in his mind, then vanished.

He now felt the bitter taste of being alone. A place he'd known from times before. Much too familiar to the old Navajo. Not the deep sadness that one feels from time to time, but an emptiness of the spirit that comes into the heart and lingers.

Peshlakai packed his bags and prepared for his trip south to Texas. He'd take his old truck to his mechanic friend. Make sure it was safe for the journey.

It would be a long ride to Palestine, but that was good. It would give him time to think. Clear his mind and his emotions. Make peace with his sister's transition to the next life.

He'd bury her with honor.

CHAPTER 3

Samantha was frustrated. She looked at the third dress she'd just tried on and it didn't feel right.

It was A-DAY at school, and she would be sitting next to Salvador in history class. They were beginning to talk more. He was even walking her to some of her classes. She tried to stay calm, but it felt like they were slowly becoming a couple.

She'd known Sal since the 9th grade. At first, he just seemed like a very angry boy. Somewhat quiet, distant, and troubled. He was kind and respectful in class to most of the teachers, but combative to those who talked down to him in any way. Or gave him a wrong look.

He was angry. He had an attitude. She wanted none of it.

But that was until last September when Sal confronted a senior boy who was harassing her in front of her locker. Grabbing her butt. Saying vulgar things to her in front of others. Spreading detailed rumors of his sexual exploits with her.

Sal had watched this unfold from a distance. Finally, he'd had enough.

"Excuse me…maybe you should keep your hands off Samantha. She's asked you several times. I'm sure you understand the English language".

The senior, almost twice his size, looked shocked, and turned his attention to Sal. He sneered, looked over at his friends, and then back to Sal.

"Look punk, mind your own business. I've been hosing this bitch for the past two…"

CRACK! Sal threw the whole weight of his body into his left fist and it landed on the boy's jaw. His right fist followed, and the boy fell to the floor.

Then Sal was on top of him, flailing and swinging both fists as hard and as fast as he could. An overwhelming rage possessed his body, coming somewhere from deep inside. His fists and arms kept punching and beating.

Suddenly, he felt a knee in the back, a foot to the head, and a heavy weight of bodies on top of him. The guy's friends had jumped in with a flurry of fists to his face. Blood was trickling out of his mouth, running down his nose. His head throbbed.

But as soon as the fight started, it was over. Two vice-principals and a security guard separated the boys. They were all escorted to the principal's office.

Sal got 3-days suspension from school. One more fight, the principal told him, and he would be kicked out permanently. In addition, he was required to see the high school counselor and create an "Anger Management Plan" to deal with his temper.

The senior boys got nothing but two days of detention and a warning to stay away from Samantha.

At that moment, Samantha became infatuated by this boy who had stood up for her. Salvador Jesus Gonzalez. Who was he, really? Why had he fearlessly tried to protect her?

September 19. In her mind, the day she first met the real Salvador. Their anniversary date. Over the next several months they began to talk. Then from time to time he'd walk her to class. And sometimes he would meet her in the morning in front of the school.

That was until Monday, April 23rd. She saw Sal and his friend Zane in front of the principal's office before 1st period. Sal was looking down, angry, frustrated. Blood coming out of his mouth. Shirt ripped. Face battered and bruised.

She found out that Sal's friend Zane was getting picked on in the bathroom before school. By the same guy and his friends who had been harassing her.

A fight ensued and continued in the hallway. A big ugly scene. The security guards were called in, and the police. Sal got three more days suspension.

The police said Sal's mom would be fined $250 by the court, and Salvador's fight would be part of a permanent police file. But the principal said that Sal would not get kicked out since witnesses stated the other boy threw the first punch.

Sal was hanging on by a thread, but he didn't give a shit.

CHAPTER 4

Sal sat on a stool at the end of the counter of the Waffle House Restaurant, his favorite spot. "Scattered, smothered, covered, chunked and diced. Jimmy Dean sausage and coffee."

It was Tuesday, day one of his 3-day *vacation*, and he felt good. Excited to have a break from school.

Marcedelia looked down at the end of the counter and saw her son. Why was he not at school? And why did he have scratches all over his face and a swollen nose? She knew the answer to the question before she asked it.

His mom had worked at the Waffle House for 10 years. Her shift was the 7am-3pm, but she would fill in at any moment for any shift. Extra pay, of course.

She was the most valuable employee at the restaurant, with the most experience and the longest tenure. A prime-time player at the Waffle House: waitress, cook, manager, bookkeeper.

A few years earlier she went to the regional boss and told him that she was only interested in being a waitress. Too many hours away from her only son who was in high school. Her son needed her there for support as he was nearing graduation.

The boss agreed to her request and gave her a raise to make sure she didn't leave.

"How many days did you get suspended for fighting?", his mom asked.

"Sorry mom, I didn't want you to worry, but this guy was picking on Zane. There was no one there to protect him. I couldn't just stand there and watch it."

Sal took a sip of coffee and continued. "The principal gave me 3-days off, and five days of anger management classes. Said he'd call you this morning for an appointment after school today."

Marcedelia sat a plate of used dishes by the sink and looked at her son. "Three days' vacation, huh?", she said sarcastically. "What are you going to do with your time?"

"Well, when I finish these awesome hash browns, I'm going to do some serious work on the '62. I think I can get it running. I know a few guys that work on these old Chevys. I'll have it humming by summer."

Sal continued talking, knowing that he had only a few minutes before his mom had to get back to her customers.

"How's Zack the jackass? Haven't seen him around lately."

"Broke up with him. Should have never started dating him, but he was persistent and I gave in. Sorry."

Sal loved his mom. She had her weakness, he had his anger. She was a good mom. He was lucky to have her.

"Mom, you're a great person. You make good hash browns too. See you at home tonight."

Marcy gave him a long, mom look. Tears slowly trickled down her cheeks. Her lips quivered.

He hesitated a few seconds, waived and walked out the door. *Where to now?*

CHAPTER 5

Out the door of the Waffle House and on his bike, Sal made his way the two miles to their mobile home. Down streets he had traveled many times.

Wind blowing through his hair, he felt a sense of freedom. He jumped the small creek, full speed. Past car lots and a tire-battery shop which was a bright yellow cinder block building with a pit-bull chained outside named *Beast*. The dog had a bad disposition.

He'd had a few run-ins with this dog, so Sal nonchalantly lifted his left hand off the bike as he was riding by and gave *Beast* the middle finger. The dog quickly lifted his head, stood and snarled, teeth flashing.

Muscles tensed on *Beast's* powerful body, and he jerked at the chain toward Sal. Sal grinned and quietly said, "Kiss my ass."

When he pulled into the gravel and grass driveway of his mobile home he looked up and saw Samantha sitting on the front doorsteps, a small grin on her face and her backpack next to her.

He stared at her much longer than was customary, then turned away quickly when she looked up.

She was beautiful. Long dark hair, deep coffee brown eyes and a jaw dropping shape. Even in faded jeans and sandals.

"Moms coming to get me in a few minutes. She said it wasn't safe to sit here long by myself. I thought you might be here and wanted to see you before…to say goodbye before you left Dallas, like you been talking about."

Samantha suddenly got quiet, her face somber. She lowered her head then looked back at Sal, trying to read what was on his mind.

Sal got off his bike and leaned it against the trailer. He walked over to the front doorsteps and slowly sat down beside Samantha. He looked out at the yard, across the street, and beyond.

He had no idea what to say. They both sat there in the mid-morning hours, looking out into the blue North Texas sky.

After a few minutes he looked over at Samantha and noticed she was wearing a silver pendant with a blue and red stone. "What's that you're wearing on your neck?"

"It's a gift from my Navajo grandmother. A pendant with turquoise and coral she got as a gift from a boy she liked on the reservation. She wore it when she was my age, said the turquoise brought her good luck. Said it would protect me and keep me in harmony with life."

He thought about that for a minute. Then he thought about his situation, suspended for fighting for three days. Not sure if he would graduate from high school.

"Maybe I need something like that. The good luck part."

"Sal, what are you going to do now?"

"Well, I think I can get the '62 Chevy running before

23

school's out, so I'll work on it the next few days. I know a few guys who work on these old Chevy's and they say they can help me."

Samantha looked at the beat-up, rusty Chevy that had been sitting there for years. "Why do you like that old junk car?"

"Mom said it belonged to dad. My real dad. Said she'd give me the original title and the car when I graduate."

She thought about asking him about the fight at school in the bathroom. She thought about telling him how she felt about him, how she was beginning to feel about him. Instead, she talked about one of their teachers.

"Mr. T asked me why you weren't in class yesterday. I told him you got in a fight. He's a crazy white dude, but cool. He said to swing by Friday morning when you get back to school, if you want to. To come early. He had something to show you."

From around the corner Samantha's mom drove up, window down. "Samantha, we've got to hurry. You've missed almost all of your first period class."

Samantha got up reluctantly, wondering if she would ever see Sal again.

"You can call me tonight if you want to. I'll let you know what you missed in class. Goodbye Salvador." She got into the car with a deep uneasy feeling inside.

Her mother drove down the potholed street, taking her away from this boy she'd begun to care deeply about. She looked back at Sal sitting on the front porch of his house, all alone. Overwhelmed by emotion, she burst into a flood of tears.

CHAPTER 6

Sal got up and walked over to the 1962 Chevy wagon. He walked around it and looked at it closely. Flat tires, rusted front floorboard, broken back window, and no battery.

His mom had parked it when he was in the 5th grade, the last time it was on the road. Last time that it had been running. That was seven years ago.

For the first time he seriously thought about his situation, and it was bleak. Seventeen-year old male. No job. No car that was running. No money. Suspended from school for the second time this year for fighting, about to get kicked out. And a record on file with the police department.

He was another statistic waiting to happen. Another Hispanic high school dropout. The kind politicians love to talk about when they speak on T.V, trying to get elected to office. The worst part about it was that he didn't really care.

School bored him, except for some teachers and a few classes. He knew he loved learning, loved reading things that interested him, but couldn't seem to get into the high school groove.

School was too restrictive, too narrow of a focus. Not enough flexibility in choosing what classes to take. Too much time spent on tests, meaningless homework, credits, more tests, preparation for tests, class rank, graduation plans, college choice, more tests.

But school would be over in a few months, if he could make it that long. And what great plan for his life did he have?

"What's up numb-nuts?" He looked up and saw his best friend Zane walking down his street and up to the car. "Lets' get this piece of shit running and go get something to eat."

Sal grinned, "It might take a while. It's been sitting for seven years. What are you doing skipping school?"

Zane was a five-foot-five African American male who weighed 125 pounds soaking wet. But he was brilliant. Lived with his grandmother. Whizzed through all the upper level math and science classes effortlessly. Was in the top ten of his class. Could have been the Val or Sal if he worked a little harder, but those titles didn't interest him.

They met the first day of the ninth grade while trying to get their class schedule. Traded insults non-stop all year, their favorite past time. They had bonded quickly and were almost inseparable.

"I picked up something for you that I found on Amazon. Ordered it last week. Something you been talkin' about for a while."

Zane took off his backpack, pulled out a package that had been opened, and threw in on the hood of the car. "Go ahead, look."

Sal picked it up, pulled out the booklet inside the package. His face beamed.

"Wow! I've been thinking about getting one of these for years. A 1962 Chevy Belaire Station Wagon manual. You rock dude! Let's see if we have enough brain cells to get this thing going."

Zane looked at his friend Sal in a rare moment of seriousness.

"Look......I know you been thinking about leaving Dallas. I was talking to Mr. T first period this morning and I told him I was coming here. I showed him what I got you. He wants you to come by Friday morning after your *vacation*, needed to see you. I told him you'd be there unless you wanted me to kick your ass."

Sal laughed. "I'll be there. I've already had my ass kicked once this week. Don't want another one by your skinny butt."

CHAPTER 7

Sal and Zane looked over the dilapidated vehicle that had sat in the yard for seven years. They made a list of all the things it needed, then wrote down the name, addresses and phone numbers of the guys who knew how to fix old Chevys. Finally, they estimated the cost of the restoration in detail.

"I'm gonna have to work and get some money to get this thing going, any type of work."

"About time you woke up to the real world, loser." Zane laughed and strapped on his backpack. "Sal, I gotta get back to school. My grandmom's picking me up at 4 and doesn't know I skipped. See you Friday."

As Zane was leaving, Sal heard his phone ring. He walked over to the front drivers' door of the Chevy, reached through the window and picked up the phone sitting on the dashboard.

"Yo, this is Sal."

"Hi Salvador. I hope I'm not calling at a bad time."

It was Samantha. His heart began to beat faster. He was excited but tried to stay calm. "All good. What's going on?"

"My mom and I are working the Canton Flea Market this

Saturday. We work it almost every Saturday. It's how I've been saving money for college. Anyway, we have some big, heavy items we can't lift into our SUV, and need someone with muscles to help. My mother will pay you $30, plus meals for the day."

Sam continued. "If it's not something you're interested in, I understand. But it might be fun. You had asked me to let you know if we ever needed some help, so I told my mom I would call you."

Sal smiled, a big warm smile. "I'm in on one condition. No pay. However, I will take any meal your mom has for us. Deal?"

"Deal. But…she may still try to pay you. You'll have to argue with her about that. Oh yea, remember that metal rock you got at a garage sale? There's a guy at the flea market that buys them, if you want some extra money. Anyway, see you at school Friday?"

"See you Friday." He put the phone down and thought about Samantha. Thought about Zane, and the '62 Chevy.

Maybe he would make it to graduation. But he wouldn't bet on it.

CHAPTER 8

There were few teachers who captured Sal's attention in school, and Mr. T was one of them. He taught History, Government and a one semester Leadership class for seniors.

Mr. T didn't look like your normal teacher. He had semi-long, unkempt hair, and wore khakis or jeans with his Merrill Moab hiking boots. A turquoise ring was on his left hand, and he wore some type of a thing around his neck people called a western tie, officially known as a bolo. Not what you see on your normal teacher in downtown Dallas. Not what he had ever seen on a teacher.

But Mr. T didn't seem to care about what others said. Or did. Or thought.

Nor did he have the usual philosophy of a teacher. On the first day of class, while giving out his syllabus and going over the rules, the 1st rule of class was that students will do all work at school.

"NO HOMEWORK. We'll complete our work in class, turn it in, then go home. You are here eight to ten hours a day, which is a typical day in the world of work. We will do the same in this class. Students DO… have a life outside of school. Seems like common sense to me. Any questions?"

Yes. Every student had questions but did not ask. They were too shocked. Was he really serious? It turns out that he was. They worked every day. They learned every day. They were respected and challenged every day. And students loved his class.

He went on. "Too much bullshit in the education system. Needs to be cleaned out. Lots of stuff going on that has nothing to do with learning and education."

"Same thing in the government. Too much bullshit! The Senate and the House of Representatives, which is supposed to represent the people of America, only represent their next election bid. We get a lot of legislation that has nothing to do with helping Americans."

****

7 am Friday, his first day back at school, and hardly anyone was in the hallway. Sal eased up to room #104 and noticed the door was open. He peeked in and saw Mr. T in the back of the room, sitting at a rickety wood table, reading by the glow of a small lamp.

Mr. T looked up. "How was the three-day vacation?" The question was followed by a deep belly laugh. "Wish I could take three days off."

"Morning Mr. T. Zane said you wanted me to come by this morning. Am I interrupting?".

He held up his coffee cup. "Komodo Dragon, great coffee from Indonesia. Smoky taste, intense, mysterious. Come on in." Mr. T motioned for Sal to take a chair.

"I'm downsizing some of my library and have a few extra

31

books from our Leadership class that you might be interested in."

Mr. T reached down and picked up two books, placed them in a well-used UT sports bag and handed them to Sal. "Here's two books I talk about a lot in class. Thought you might like them. May be helpful when you graduate in a few months."

Sal eagerly took the bag without looking at the books. "Thanks Mr. T, you da man."

Mr. T continued. "You missed a movie we watched in class while you were gone this week. *Kung Fu, 1972*. Here's the handout with the questions, and the video. Maybe you can watch it this weekend and bring it back on Monday. We'll talk about it."

"Will do." Sal got up to leave and Mr. T followed.

"One more thing. Take this." Mr. T handed him a one-dollar bill. "Flip it over on the back. Look at the writing above the eagle: *E PLURIBUS UNUM*. It's a Latin phrase. Try to find out what it means and why it might be important…as an American, as a human. Happy trails."

Sal hesitated before leaving. "Mr. T, you never told us what the "T" means, have you?"

"See you Monday, grasshopper." He laughed as Sal walked out the door, down the dark empty hallway.

Sal felt light, hopeful. He might make it to graduation.

CHAPTER 9

Sal's alarm went off at 4:30 am. Shower, dress, and out the door. As he was leaving he picked up the metal rock displayed on his dresser and put it in his pocket. He wasn't sure exactly what fascinated him about the rock, other than it had a cool *vibe*.

Quietly he exited the trailer and locked the door behind him, careful not to wake his mom. He jumped on his bike and cruised down the dark streets of his neighborhood, passing several cars with party music blasting out of their windows.

Over the bridge that spanned highway 175, he rode on till he arrived at Samantha's apartment complex and eased through the parking lot. A few guys hanging out eyeballed him suspiciously.

As he walked up to her apartment, he encountered Sam's mom, Angela, who was carrying a box of merchandise to the vehicle. "Morning Salvador, glad you're able to help us today. Looks like we will have to put the antique dresser on top. Almost everything else is ready to go."

After securing the dresser, Angela eased the Suburban

onto highway 175, then picked up I-20 heading east to Canton.

Three people fit snuggly in the front seat, and Sal could feel Sam's legs pressing against his. Instinctually he turned toward her, admiring the shimmering brown hair that fell effortlessly upon her shoulders.

Feeling his glance, she looked up and smiled. He grinned sheepishly and looked away, his heart pounding.

They took the *First Monday* exit off I-20 and continued traveling down a two-lane country road until they arrived at the entrance. "Mornin' mam, I need to see your dealer permit." Angela showed the gate keeper her One-Day Dealer Pass, and they were waved in.

Samantha had made an attempt to describe her experience of Canton, but Sal was still overwhelmed by his first glimpse.

He'd never seen such a conglomeration of stuff for sale, packed in old rattle-trap pickups and beat up cars. U-Haul trailers stacked fifteen feet high rumbled precariously over pot-holed asphalt. Junk cars with busted out back windows. Fancy RV's up to 50-feet long. Guys riding bicycles and golf carts filled with junk metal and badly damaged antiques.

Angela maneuvered through the narrow asphalt paths till she found their two spaces, U-55, U-56. "The antique dealers from Houston and Dallas are already pickin', so let's hurry and get set up. Then you and Sal can go get something to eat."

"Remember mom, Salvador is a rookie. I told him we would be easy on him." Sam and her mom laughed.

"Bring it on", said Sal. He joined the laughter and the unpacking began.

Thirty minutes later they were ready for business. Samantha walked over to Salvador, grabbed his hand and gave it a gentle squeeze. "Time for breakfast...back in a little bit mom."

Sal felt the warmth and softness of Sam's hand. Saw the simple beauty in her smile. He looked around at the open-air market as the vendors moved about, and watched the open blue skies give way to a rising Texas sun. A sense of magic had descended upon the fields of Canton.

After a brief stroll they followed the savory smells of bacon toward a small breakfast tent, Gil's. They waited in line several minutes, listening to a small group of dealers' hurl insults affectionately at each other.

The line moved on and Sam stepped up to the counter. "We'd like two orders of the 'Breakfast Special' for here, and one order to go. Along with three coffees."

After breakfast they worked their way through the gathering crowd and back to their space, where Angela was in the middle of a negotiation.

"Sir, I can't take less than $80 for the chair, but I thank you for the $5 offer."

"No...no....no...I can't give a penny more than $10," replied the potential customer whose face had turned to anguish. Angela smiled as the man walked away mumbling under his breath, empty handed.

The day went by quickly, with conversations of buying and selling and trading. And of treasures excavated out of piles of junk and sold on *Antiques Road Show* for thousands. And of slow sales and no sales. The big deal that got away.

As the day moved on, Sal became fascinated by the ritual of negotiation. Every customer, it seemed, tried to lower the price of an item by offering far less than the merchandise was worth. The back-and-forth exchange was like watching a game of tennis. Offer-Counter Offer...Counter-Counter Offer...and so on.

Salvador soon found himself thrust into the mix of this mayhem with a trade of his own. It centered around the metal rock that he bought months ago at a garage sale for $1. Turned out the rock had some value. How much, he was unsure.

"This is him Sal. I know you've never done this before, but you'll get the hang of it. Just show him what you have and see if he wants to buy it. That'll get the ball rollin'. I'll be here if you need help."

Sal pulled the rock from his pocket and awkwardly approached the dealers table. "Sir, my friend said you might have some interest in this metal rock." Sal handed the dealer the rock.

The dealer took the rock and quickly identified it as a meteorite. He examined it closely before placing it on a small scale. Then, not wanting to disclose his interest or tell the kid his rock was a meteorite, he casually handed it back to Sal.

"Yea, I occasionally buy rocks like these, but I don't give much for 'em. I'd say it's worth about five bucks." The dealer tried to conceal his excitement, but Samantha noticed immediately. She'd worked the market every weekend since the seventh grade.

Sam looked at Sal and he read her face: *It's worth more than $5.* The dealer, sensing a hesitation, quickly changed his strategy.

"Tell you what...I'll go against my better judgement and give you $15 for the rock. That's my best cash price! Or...", he pointed toward a small box close by, "I can trade you straight across for *one* item in this small wooden box, if you see something that catches your eye."

Sal brushed his hand through the small collection of used silver jewelry in the box, trying to find something he liked.

Most of it was damaged or broken, *except* for one piece.

"Can I look at that turquoise ring?"

Sal took the ring from the dealer and looked at it closely. The deep blue color of the stone pulled Sal into its spell. Set in aged silver, he felt as if he were holding a piece of ancient treasure.

"Do you like it Sal?" Samantha smiled and cocked her head at him inquisitively.

He looked at Samantha, unsure what to do next.

Noticing Sal's hesitation, Sam stepped up to the table confidently and looked dead-eyed into the face of the merchant. "We'll give you the rock, in exchange for the turquoise ring AND twenty dollars. Otherwise, we'll take it to a dealer inside the Convention Center and see what he will offer for it."

Samantha waited only a few seconds before reaching out her hand to pick up the meteorite.

The dealer quickly changed tactics. "Weeeellllll...I don't know. Sounds a little steep." He shifted uneasily. "I guess I'll go ahead and give you the ring and $20, since your friend seems to like it. I just hope I don't get beat up too much more today, or I'll be in the poor house."

Sam looked at Sal, rolled her eyes, then turned back to the dealer with a pleasant smile. She spoke slowly, respectfully. "Thank you, sir."

The dealer picked up the meteorite and smiled, concealing his anger. *If that damn girl hadn't jumped in I would have got the meteorite for almost nothing.* However, he knew it's value. The meteorite would easily bring $300 at the Tucson Gem and Mineral Show in February.

Samantha grabbed Sal's hand and grinned as they left the booth. "Not bad for your first trade."

Salvador flashed a puzzled look at Sam. "How'd you do that?"

"Do what?", Sam asked innocently.

He smiled. "You know what I mean. How did you know the metal rock had value? And how did you get the dealer to give me the ring...and $20?"

Sam laughed loudly, playfully. "I have no idea what you're talking about."

Salvador's heart pounded as he looked at the radiance on her face. He moved closer, wrapped both arms around her and lifted her gently into the air.

"You're making fun of me cause I'm a rookie."

Her laughter echoed in the air as he spun her around. Then, without warning, their eyes met. She eased her hands around his neck and pulled him close against her body, never taking her eyes off his eyes.

After what seemed like several minutes, Sam released him from her embrace. "Mom's probably wondering where we are. We better go."

Before long they were packing the Suburban in preparation for the ride home.

"Samantha", Angela said while she was organizing the unsold merchandise in the back seat of the Suburban, "I forgot to tell you that I got a call yesterday from someone who I used to know a long time ago, one of my first real boyfriends. I hadn't heard from him in years. He was extremely helpful during a difficult time in my life. Got me out of a big mess."

Angela continued: "He said he's driving through Dallas tonight on his way to Nevada and wanted to know if it would be alright to stop by and say hi, see how things are going with me."

Sam looked at her mom quizzically. "You've never told me

about him, have you?"

"No. It was a guy I met not long after I graduated from high school, and to be honest, I was crushed when he broke up with me. Anyway, I gave him our address. He said he's driving a red Corvette. We'll make a place for him to stay on the couch if he gets in too late and needs to rest. I owe him that much."

Sam was puzzled, and curious. She'd never heard of this man, but she had learned to trust her mom. She'd ask questions later when they got home.

In the meantime, she had something special she wanted to give Sal before they finished for the day, something she'd been thinking about all week. Her instincts told her the time was right. She knew he was falling for her.

"Come on Sal. Let's get a corndog and a coke for the ride home."

They walked up to the window of a makeshift wooden corndog stand and ordered. When their food arrived, Sam led Sal to an outdoor table by the stand.

Sal began to eat his corndog while Sam fumbled around in her purse, pulling out an old silver bracelet. Real old. With a crudely cut green piece of turquoise in the center of the bracelet. She sat the bracelet in the center of the table.

"Wow!", he said, his mouth still full. "Where'd you get that?"

"I got it in a trade with a guy from Arizona several years ago who used to have a trading post in the Four Corners area of New Mexico. Picked up about twenty pieces from him, and this is the only one I have left."

Samantha gently picked up the bracelet, looked into Sal's face and handed it to him, tears building in her brown eyes.

"Your gift for helping us today." She couldn't hold it in any longer. He had to know how she felt about him. "I love you Salvador."

Sal was speechless. Slowly, he placed the old bracelet on his wrist and reached for Samantha's hand, caressing it gently. The two teens sat motionless, eyes locked in a trance.

"OK love birds," Angela was smiling. "the suns about to set and we have to get home."

As they traveled west toward Dallas, *Sal looked down at the old bracelet on his wrist. He ran his hand across the silver and examined the stone, hoping the luck in the turquoise would help get him to graduation.*

CHAPTER 10

Fifty-year old James Benson had made a lot of money in Pensacola, Florida over the past two decades. Some great real estate deals, and some wise investments.

But trouble was on his trail. Trouble with women. All ages of women. Young, old, and of every nationality. He thought about the beauty of the female body night and day. Soon his drive for sex overwhelmed him. Engulfed him. Dominated his thoughts. And it pushed him to leave Florida in the middle of the night.

Through the years the police had been in contact with him about his escapades in the bars of Pensacola. Stalking women. Riding the edge of the law in satisfying his sexual desires. And about his photography of young girls on the beaches, his advances toward underaged females, and his sexual conquests.

But no one had ever pressed charges. None of the girls were willing to testify against him until now. The girl, a 15-year old he'd met on an isolated beach named Jasmine. Wild and beautiful. He'd photographed her extensively. Had sex with her.

The most dangerous part about the situation was that her father had found out and wanted justice. Street justice. He was out for blood.

Jasmine's father, a special forces operative on assignment in Afghanistan, would be arriving home in a few days, on leave for a month.

During his last phone call with his wife, he found out about his daughter's meetings with James. Found out he'd taken hundreds of pictures of Jasmine in her bikini on the beach. But when he discovered they'd had sex, he flew into a fit of rage.

"Put Jasmine on the phone!", he yelled. Jasmine's mother handed her the phone. "Tell me about this scum bag piece of shit you been seeing!! And you tell that worthless piece of trash that when I get home, I'm gonna..."

He grilled her with questions until she sobbed uncontrollably, dropped the phone, and ran into her bedroom.

Secretly, Jasmine worried about what her father would do to James when he got back to the states, so she called to warn him. Told him that her father had found out about their 'meetings' and was coming after him.

She said her father would be *undercover, fully armed, and vowed to take care of the situation on his own personal time, as soon as his plane hit the ground.*

So fifty-year old Florida real estate agent James Benson decided to move to Las Vegas. He could get lost in that world and make great money in the real estate market. No one would find him.

While he was packing the last of his stuff to leave, he came across some old pictures with names and addresses and phone numbers.

One of them was an old girlfriend he'd had a brief fling with. *Great piece of ass.* The picture showed them in bathing suits on a south Florida beach. He called. She answered. Now he was on his way to see her. Interstate 10 west all the way to Houston. Then north on I-45 to Dallas where Angela waited.

He was flush in cash years ago when they were dating and had given her several thousand dollars to get out of a situation. *She owed him, big time. He would collect tonight.*

She said she didn't have a husband or a steady boyfriend, just her and her teenage daughter. *Easy to maneuver the kid out of the way so he could have some fun with mom. He was getting excited at the thoughts going through his mind.*

CHAPTER 11

James pulled into Angela's apartment around midnight Saturday, grabbed a beer out of his cooler and relaxed. He was anticipating a night of pleasure. Maybe a little breakfast in the morning, then on to his new life in Vegas.

He knocked on the apartment door and she appeared, her thin robe unable to conceal the outline of her breasts. "Hi James. It's been a long, long time. Come on in." He followed her in, never taking his eyes off her hips. He strained to see through her gown.

"I've got your couch ready. Sheets, pillows, and blankets. Your bathroom is just a few feet away, past the T.V."

She slowly approached him as he sat his suitcase by the couch. "I'm sorry I won't be able to stay up and talk tonight. I've worked all day and am exhausted. My boss called me and said he needed me to fill in for the early shift tomorrow morning."

Angela noticed the disappointment in his face but continued. "I'll never forget how you helped me out all those years ago. It's one of the nicest things anyone has ever done for me. But if you are still here when I get off work tomorrow maybe we can catch up. A few of my friends are coming over and they would love to meet you."

"One last thing. My daughter usually gets up on Sunday around 11am. She'll be happy to cook you a late breakfast if you haven't left for Vegas. Goodnight James."

Damn! Ungrateful bitch! He had no intention of laying around Dallas and meeting her friends. He just wanted to *hit it* and get on to Vegas where there were a lot of beautiful women.

Nothing he could do now but sleep a few hours and get on down the road.

****

James woke up late Sunday morning, frustrated with the events from the night before. And his back ached from the lumpiness of the sofa. He sat up and looked around the room. What time was it anyway? Time to roll.

That's when he heard a door open behind him and turned around. Samantha walked in.

Long, golden brown legs exposed up to her hips. Beautiful dark hair hanging loosely down her back. She wore a short nighty, and walked over to the front door, unaware of the man on the couch leering at her.

She unlocked the door, cracked it open, then slowly walked back to the refrigerator.

She's teasing me, he thought.

Sam began to get out eggs and bacon for breakfast. Suddenly she reached way up in the cabinet above to get the bread, exposing her panties and her tight butt cheeks.

She had to know he was watching. She must be horny. She wants me. She wants it.

"Good morning", he said.

Startled, Samantha turned and looked at James in surprise. She was embarrassed. She put her arms in front of her body, trying to hide her exposed cleavage.

"Oh…good morning." Then she remembered. "You must be my mom's friend from Florida." She felt nervous. She noticed him starring at her body.

"Yea, we were close years ago. Hate to miss talking with your mom," he lied, "but I'm gonna have to leave in about an hour. She said you wouldn't mind cooking me some breakfast before I left. I see you're getting that all ready."

Samantha felt her heart pounding with fear. She heard herself say: "Uhhhh…sure. Let me go wash up and I'll come back and make you something."

That's when James quickly got up from the couch and approached with only his underwear on. *She froze in fear as he got close, an evil smirk on his face.*

He'd had enough of these games. She wanted it, like all the young girls he'd been with in Florida. They pretended to be afraid, but in reality they just wanted a man with a strong hand who was willing to take what he wanted.

She backed against the kitchen counter, trapped. He came closer and closer, his eyes crazed. Then he grabbed her and pressed his body firmly against hers.

With his knee he pried open her legs. His right hand grabbed the back of her hair, and with his left hand he grabbed her panties and pulled downward.

At that point she screamed and scratched wildly at his eyes with her fingernails. Blood poured down his face and stained her white nightgown.

Then he was all over her. She couldn't move. His massive chest pinned her against the kitchen counter. His hands roamed her body at will. *She couldn't believe this was happening to her.*

CHAPTER 12

Sal stayed up late Saturday night after Sam's mom dropped him off from the flea market, completing the assignment Mr. T had given him.

This was his kind of homework. Watch an old vintage movie from the '70's. Fill out the questions on the worksheet. Turn them in Monday. The theme of the movie seemed to be 'CHEE', inner strength. Life's tough, so you got to be mentally tough to survive.

Suddenly his phone rang. "Good morning Salvador." It was Samantha.

Sal's heart skipped a beat. "Morning Sam. Got my bracelet on. Feels good, like it's got its own energy."

"Glad you like it. Didn't know if you've eaten yet, but if you're hungry and want to come over, I'll cook you a late breakfast. About 11:30." She continued, "Mom will be getting off by the time we finish eating and wanted to talk to you about working with us at the flea market on Saturday for the next several weeks. That is, if you liked it."

"So, you know how to cook breakfast?" he teased. "What's

on the menu?"

"Well…we got eggs with Hatch green chili peppers, bacon, toast…and coffee. Does that sound ok?"

"I'm there. See you soon." Sal hung up the phone and took a deep breath. He couldn't stop thinking about Samantha.

Was it Love? He had no idea since he'd never been in love. There were a few girls he'd liked through the years, but he'd never had a steady girlfriend.

He was momentarily lost in his thoughts 'til he looked at the clock in his bedroom. 11:15 am. "Coffee time!", he said aloud. In minutes he was out the door and on his bike, cruising swiftly through his neighborhood. Across the freeway and down a few more blocks until he arrived at Samantha's apartment.

As he got off his bike, he noticed the front door was cracked open. And then he heard a loud scream from inside the apartment. It was Samantha.

Instinctually, he dropped his bike and rushed through the front door, shocked at the scene before him. Sam's nightgown was covered in blood, and a stocky suntanned man, dressed only in his underwear, was brutally pressing his body against hers.

With a fury and intensity he was unconscious of, Salvador ripped the man away from her and violently threw him to the ground. And then he was on top of him, pounding his fists into the face of the attacker with a bitterness he'd never experienced. His hands and arms worked like a sledgehammer, pulverizing the attacker's face till he was unrecognizable.

The man stopped moving, but not Salvador. He beat him until the blood covered the floor around him, and still he couldn't stop.

"Sal!!...Stop!!...You're going to kill him! He's not moving!"

Sal slowed his fists, then stopped. He was breathing hard and shaking, staring at the bloodied mess of a man underneath him.

In the distance he heard Samantha crying. Slowly, he came to his senses. "Samantha...you all right?" He walked over and put his arms around her. She sobbed louder, deeper.

"Yes...I'm ok." Her voice was shaking. "It's that friend my mom used to know a long time ago. He must have gotten in late last night."

She continued to cry for another few minutes, then took a deep breath. "I didn't know he was here, and when I got up to start cooking your breakfast he spoke to me. I was shocked to see him. He kept staring at me. Then, he started walking toward me...and...". Sam started crying again.

After a few minutes Salvador looked down at the man, wondering if he was breathing. Fully aware now, he picked up his phone and dialed 911. "Hello, there's a person here that's hurt really bad. I'm not sure if he's breathing. The address is..."

Unknown to Salvador and Samantha, a man in sunglasses stood just a few inches from the open front door, quietly watching the scene before him.

The man stood 5'11" and stacked 190 pounds of solid muscle on his sturdy frame. He wore a white t-shirt with Cancun written on the front, a Dallas Cowboys cap, army fatigue pants and combat boots.

On his left arm a big tattoo displayed the name JASMINE.

CHAPTER 13

In the dimly lit basement of the police station, Salvador sat handcuffed to a table. He could hear the beating of his heart.

Was this the end of the road? Would he receive a long prison sentence for killing a man? Did his anger finally get the best of him?

The door opened and two men entered. One in full police uniform, the other in casual business attire. The policeman sat in the far corner of the room. The other man, who appeared to be a detective, sat across from him. He placed a folder on the table, opened it up and flipped through the file.

"The man you attacked is in critical condition. These pictures in your file reveal one of the most brutal beatings I've ever seen." The detective flipped through the rest of the file, then closed it.

"But that's not all. Your file also says that you have had TEN major fights since you entered high school, and you've been suspended seven times. Does that sound about right?"

Sal swallowed, breathed deeply and responded. "Yes sir."

There was a knock at the door. The detective and the policeman both got up and walked out. Sal could faintly hear several men talking with the detective in the hallway.

In the quietness and solitude of the moment, a darkness descended upon Salvador. He felt tears welling up in his eyes. He would be going to jail for a long time.

The two men re-entered the room.

The detective appeared puzzled. He looked at Sal, leaned back in his chair and rubbed his chin. "Gonzalez...I don't know how you got out of this but let me give you a quick update. Your bail was set at $100,000 and...let's just say someone well connected walked in and paid it. You'll be processed out in the next few hours, given a court date, and released. Your mother is waiting in the lobby."

The detective got up and walked to the door. The policeman grabbed Sal's arm and followed. Before they left the room, the detective turned to look at Sal.

"Your court date will be set within the next week or two. Make sure you're there." The detective continued. "I wouldn't get too comfortable if I was you. As I told you, the man you brutally beat is in critical condition. If he dies, you won't see the light of day for another 25 years. Got it?"

Sal lowered his head and nodded.

CHAPTER 14

Marcy had been crying for most of the morning, but there were no tears left. Her son had beaten a man to within an inch of his life. And though it was in defense of another person, the extent of the beating was of grave concern to the police department. He could be facing years in prison.

And there was another burden she'd carried. It was a secret about Sal's real father she'd kept from her son. A secret hidden in a box and stashed away in the closet of her bedroom.

She told herself she was trying to protect him but knew that was untrue. He no longer believed her lies about his father. Hadn't believed them in years.

Marcy got up from her bed, went to the bathroom and washed her face. She walked slowly to the closet in her bedroom and pushed aside several boxes of clothes.

With a screwdriver she pried open a small part of the floor, revealing a cardboard box. She lifted the box, put the sectioned piece of floor back into place, and pushed the boxes of clothes on top.

She sat on the edge of her bed, thumbing through the

contents of the box. Reliving the memories of a brief but intense romance with a young foreign archaeologist, Salvador's father. Finally, she took a deep breath and walked to the living room, placing the box on the kitchen table.

Marcy closed her eyes and prayed for strength, unsure why she'd kept the secret for so long.

But the truth was in front of her now. Crystal clear. Crises had a way of clearing the fog of deception. Maybe she thought if Sal had known who his real father was, he might have left her when he came of age.

Her conscience was screaming at her now. *Marcy, you were insecure years ago and couldn't bear the idea of not having a husband, and of losing your only son. You could not endure the idea of living life alone.*

"Morning mom." Salvador walked over and gave his mom a hug.

She smiled, then started softly crying again. "I'll pour you some coffee son. Why don't you sit down and eat your breakfast, then we'll go over our game plan for your court appearance."

Surprisingly, Sal had slept well, and the sausage smelled good. Jimmy Dean had never let him down.

"Son, I'm proud of you for protecting Samantha. If you had not been there, who knows what would have happened to her."

She picked up her coffee, took a long sip and gently placed it back on the table. "When we go to court and the judge calls you up to the front, you only need to do one thing. Tell the truth. Nothing else. You were protecting the girl you love from a man who was physically attacking her."

"I will." Sal pushed away his empty plate and picked up his coffee. "Mom, the detective who interviewed me at the police station said that if that guy dies, I could get 25 years in prison."

Sal shook his head, unable to mentally process that many years in prison, yet knowing it was a possibility. "Mom, it doesn't make sense. 25 years for protecting Samantha."

"You're right son, it doesn't make sense. A lot of life doesn't make sense. But we will go through this together, one day at a time. Remember, you only have one job when you stand in front of the judge. Tell the truth."

Their talk was interrupted by a loud motorcycle pulling up in their front yard. Sal jumped up and ran out the door. Mr. T sat on his Harley by the curb. Seeing Sal, he cut off the cycle and stepped into the front yard.

"Heard you had a little trouble yesterday," Mr. T said. "So, I decided to ride over and see how you're doing."

Sal laid out the details of his situation. Mr. T nodded, took Sal by the arm and led him several feet away.

"A local detective came by my house yesterday, a friend of your mom's. We talked for more than an hour about your situation. I liked him, and I trust him. He's got a lot of connections that could be helpful."

"Was his name Troy?"

"Yea, that was it. Said he's been digging into the case for your mom since the day you got arrested. He found out that someone high up in the department is out to get you. Tryin' to send you to jail, but he wasn't sure why. I asked him a lot of questions, but he couldn't give me any details."

Sal nodded. "Yea, the detective told me I could be heading to prison."

Mr. T lowered his voice and moved closer to Sal. "Zane came by my room after school yesterday, said you were thinking about skipping your court date and leaving town. That true?"

"I'm think'in about it because I didn't do anything wrong. This whole thing's bullshit. I don't trust those cops who arrested me, and I don't trust that detective."

"I'm with you on that. There seems to be something fishy goin' on. And I can't blame you for thinking about leaving town."

Mr. T hesitated, grasping for the right words to say. He knew this might be the last time he spoke to Sal in a long time. "I just want to make sure you think this thing all the way through. Then, if you still feel like you need to hit the road, well…"

Mr. T extended his hand toward Sal. *As they shook hands, Sal felt a small envelop pressed into his palm.* He took it and slipped it into his back pocket. Mr. T looked around the trailer park, then back at Sal.

"Read this as soon as I leave, by yourself. It's got the name and location of a close friend of mine in Dallas that you can trust, just in case you decide to head out. He'll make sure you're safe. Just don't show anybody this letter. Not Zane. Not Samantha. Not your mom. Take care Salvador."

CHAPTER 15

Marcy never got the chance that morning to open up about Sal's real dad. And the contents in the box.

Instead, she received a call from her friend Troy, one of her longtime customers at the Waffle House whom she'd been confiding in. "Marcy, I just stumbled across some new information about Sal. I'm at the restaurant, and I need to see you. When can you get here?"

"I'm on my way."

Marcy arrived at the restaurant within the hour and rushed inside toward the last booth. Troy stood up when she approached, gave her a hug, and motioned for the waitress to bring another cup of coffee.

Troy was a thirty-year veteran detective in Dallas who knew his way around. It had taken him decades to learn who to talk to, and who to avoid. He valued honesty and loyalty above all else and had developed a close friendship with Marcy. Her son was in serious trouble, and she had no one else to turn to.

"I've been digging around at the police station, trying to

find out what the hell is going on. I knew something wasn't right with this case, but I couldn't put it all together until a few hours ago."

He took an unhurried sip of coffee and continued. "The judge assigned to Sal's assault case was placed there by a high-ranking member of the police department, AND a small group of *political donors* with lots of money. They want the judge to crack down on ALL physical assault crimes in Dallas, and the perpetrators sent to prison. They want CONVICTIONS, the more the better. If the judge is seen as a crime fighter, he's got a good shot at being re-elected."

"But Troy, Sal was protecting Samantha from being raped!", Marcy exclaimed.

Troy clasped his hands together on the table. "Marcy, they don't give a damn about Sal. To them he's just another poor Hispanic kid from the hood who lives with a single mom. Trailer trash. No one will give two-shits if he goes to jail, and it looks like that's where he's headin'. Him, and a lot of other kids."

Troy hesitated, then continued. "Basically, Sal's getting' railroaded by a few corrupt assholes who want to stay in power."

Marcy buried her head and sobbed. Troy got up from his side of the booth and sat by Marcy, putting his arm around her. It took several minutes until she raised her head and looked at Troy.

"I guess I should tell you that I overheard Sal talking with Zane on the phone. He's thinking about leaving town, skipping his court date. Traveling as far away from Dallas as he can." She stared straight ahead, numb. "I don't know what to do."

Troy looked out the window, disgusted by the actions of a

tiny group of crooked cops at the police department. And a corrupt judge propped up by dirty money wreaking havoc on a young boys' life, and the life of his mother. He reached out his hand and placed it on Marcy's.

"Marcy, I've never told anyone to break the law, but if Sal's really planning on leaving, he'd better leave soon."

Marcy looked confused. "Why?"

"That'll give him a few extra days to get as far away as possible. It'll give him an edge. Because once they find out he's skipped town, they'll be coming for him."

Troy slid out of the booth and stood at the edge of the table.

"Tell you what. Why don't you go home, sit Salvador down and tell him the truth about his situation. As much as you can. Then bring him here for an early dinner, about 4pm. I'll be here and we'll talk about his case. I'll answer any questions he has. And if he is dead set on leaving, we can at least try to help him be as safe as possible." Troy walked out to his truck and drove away.

Marcy sat motionless. She rolled the information around in her mind for an hour, trying to create a plan. *How was she was going to tell her son something like this, on what could be their last dinner together? But she had no choice. And little time. He had to know today. About his legal situation, and about his real father.*

59

CHAPTER 16

Marcy arrived home to find her son working on the old Chevy. She loved the car like Sal, but for a different reason. It was really her father's car that she received as a gift when she graduated from high school, so she'd have to clear that up with him also.

She walked over to her son and put her arm around him. "The cars starting to look good son. It's going to be beautiful when you and Zane finish with it."

Sal grinned and Marcy continued. "I need you to come inside. There's something important I need to share with you. Two things. It can't wait. I'll have a cold coke sitting on the kitchen table after you clean up."

Sal immediately sensed the urgency in his mom's voice. She rarely spoke to him with that tone.

He stopped working on the car, went inside and sat at the kitchen table. His mom walked over, moved a chair to within a few inches from Sal, and looked into the eyes of her only son.

Marcy took a deep breath and began. "Son, you may hate me for what I've got to tell you. I'll understand. But I need to tell you the truth about your father. I know you haven't believed me in years."

She explained briefly how she'd met Sal's dad while vacationing with her family when she was 19. They were visiting Mexico and staying in a small motel on the island of Isla Mujeras. It was the second day of the vacation, and she was sitting with her parents on the patio of a tiny pizza cabana.

And that's when he walked by. Medium to small build, tan, ruggedly handsome. She was attracted instantly. He smiled. She smiled. And the island winds blew across their bodies, infected their souls, followed by a brief but secret romance.

"He was from Istanbul, studying to be an archaeologist," Marcy said timidly. "It's all here, sitting on the table…letters, pictures, and a few mementos he'd picked up from archaeological sites." She slid the box toward Sal.

Sal felt a lump in his throat. He slowly reached for the box, tears streaming down his face. Anger bubbled up inside after years of lies he'd endured, but it only masked a deeper pain. *How could his mom lie to him about his father?*

Marcy watched Sal's body tense up, and his tears fall on the box. "I'm sorry son. I'm ashamed that I lied to you for all these years. I hope you can forgive me. If not now, then maybe in a few years. There's no excuse for what I've done."

Sal took a deep breath, wiped his eyes and somehow reached his hands across the table, placing them on his mom's trembling hands. Then, lifting his eyes, he spoke straight from the heart. "It's ok mom…you did the best you could."

Marcy's lips quivered and the tears flowed, but she steeled herself to deliver part two of the message. Her son was on verge of going to jail for 25 years, and the situation demanded action, not emotion.

"Son…before you open the box, I need to tell one more

thing. When you got arrested, I asked Troy to look into your case at the police station, and he's found out some new information that you need to know. He wants us to meet him for dinner tonight at 4:00 pm. I told him we'd be there."

CHAPTER 17

Troy's Ford pickup was out front when they pulled into the parking lot and entered the restaurant. They walked over to his booth and sat down.

"Sal, your mom's worried to death about your upcoming court appearance, and she ask me if I would look into it. She also knows you been thinking about skipping your court date and leaving town."

"Yea," Sal nodded. "I been thinking about it, cause this whole thing just don't make sense. All I did was protect my girlfriend. Maybe I overreacted, but I'd beat his ass again in a heartbeat."

Troy nodded. "Yea, I understand. I'd probably feel the same way if I was you. Tell you what, let's go ahead and eat dinner and you can ask me anything you want to know about your case. After we eat, I'd like to talk with you privately in my pickup for a few minutes, if that's alright with your mom."

Sal asked many questions at dinner, as did his mom. Once the conversation played out Troy slid out of the booth. "I'll see you in my truck in a few minutes."

Sal made his way to Troy's truck and opened the passenger side door. Country music poured out from the cab: *'But I wonder now, if it makes a difference, does Fort Worth ever cross your mind.'*

Troy cut off the radio, looked over the dashboard and into the thick stand of trees across the parking lot.

"Sal, I always go fishing before I make a big decision. It helps me clear my mind. Relax. Put things in perspective. Grab a Zebco and cast out on an East Texas pond early in the morning. But we don't have time for that now."

Then Troy turned around and faced Sal squarely. "Word down at the station is that you're a folk hero among the police officers, and they're pissed off that some of the higher ups in the department are planning to send you to the big house. That sumbitch you beat up had a file in Florida documenting some sketchy activity with women, and they're tryin' to keep a lid on that."

"But…the only opinion that matters is the one from the judge they assigned to you. I found out the name of the judge, and it ain't good. Turns out he's trying to make a name for himself."

Troy reached out to the dashboard of his truck and picked up a can of Copenhagen. He pinched out a small dip, then placed it back.

While Troy was situating the snuff, Sal looked down and noticed a small gun holstered on the side of Troy's waist. On the back window of the cab was a gun rack with two fishing poles and a rifle.

Troy continued. "The people who got the judge his job said he had to get tough on violent crime. Told him to make an example out of you. Put you away for a long time."

Troy hesitated, watching Sal digest the information. "Any

questions?"

Sal looked at Troy intently: "Troy, would you leave town if you were me?"

"That's a tough one...but, if I was facing prison time for protecting my girlfriend from that sorry sumbitch from Florida, I'd probably consider it. Where're you thinking about goin'?"

"Not sure. Got one contact that might help me out, but don't know much about him."

Troy nodded. "Sal, if you're thinking about takin off, it's good to know that Dallas has a lot of unmarked dirt trails in the underbelly of the city, and they crisscross the Trinity River. It's a great place to disappear, but not a safe place to linger. Lots of predators, homeless, alcoholics, drug addicts, gang members, and guys trying to hide from the law."

Troy opened his glove box, pulled out a map of Dallas and pointed out exactly where the trails were. He then pointed out a few landmarks, how the Trinity flows through Dallas, and how to get out of town without getting arrested.

"I can't tell you what to do, but this might come in handy if you decide to leave." He handed the map to Sal.

Sal took the map and noticed that Troy had put some money inside. "Thanks Troy. Take care of mom if I leave. I'll be in touch."

Sal exited the cab of the pickup and made his way to his mom's car.

The ride home was quiet. His mind was spinnin' with the realities of life coming at him from every direction.

CHAPTER 18

Salvador woke early from a restless night and sat on the edge of his bed. The new revelations from his mom and Troy played over and over in his mind.

One thing seemed certain: he was heading to prison UNLESS…he took things into his own hands.

Troy wouldn't tell him what to do, but he did give him a map he could use to maneuver through the city if he decided to leave.

Mr. T had also given him a map, with the name and location of a person that he'd known for years. Sal highlighted the name of this man who could assist him on his flight from the metroplex.

What was there to lose? If he was charged with murder and got 25 years in prison, he'd never get that part of his life back. But if he left town and they caught him in a year or two, then gave him 25 years, he'd at least have experienced some life while a young man.

Bottom line, he was going to be put away for political reasons, not for justice. He'd just got caught in a web of forces that had nothing to do with protecting Samantha.

Salvador looked at the clock. 5:00 am. *If he was going to disappear, he had to leave soon. He needed the extra time to get distance between him and the law.*

Sal bolted out of bed and opened his backpack. Grabbed the two books from Mr. T, a few pair of shorts, a pair of jeans, a long sleeve shirt, a few t-shirts, underwear and socks and stuffed them inside. Along with his toothbrush and toothpaste.

He picked up *THE BOX* his mom had given him and maneuvered it inside a small compartment of his backpack. He decided not to go through the contents of the box last night. There would be time for that later.

This morning his mom's concealment of the story about his real father did not seem too important.

25 years in prison did.

In a few hours he'd be gone. On a path that led to an unknown future. Traveling down a road he knew nothing about. All he knew was that he had to leave Dallas. Fast.

There was a knock on his bedroom door. "Sal, it's mom. You all right?" She'd worried all night, wondering if her son would still be here in the morning.

"Come on in mom."

She entered, looked around the room, and knew he'd made his decision. "I'll have breakfast ready in fifteen minutes." No time for lingering or small talk, she thought. He'd set his course, and she would support him. And be strong, at least until he left.

Sal stood, strapped on his backpack, and placed the old native bracelet he'd got from Sam on his wrist. *He touched the turquoise, hoping it would bring him luck.* Hoping he would be able to come back to his mom. And his friend Zane. And Samantha.

The scent of sausage seeped under the door, calling him.

One last look around his room. He was surprised that he felt reluctant to leave this tiny space that a few weeks earlier had seemed like a prison.

Finally, he opened the door of his bedroom and walked into the kitchen. Sitting at the table, he watched his mom busy cooking his last meal. Maybe his favorite meal, breakfast. She moved with purpose and confidence.

He was lucky to have her and felt guilty he had taken for granted all the sacrifices and small kindnesses she'd lavished on him. He would soak in these last few moments.

She placed the plate in front of him, a work of art. He devoured the contents and sat back with his coffee.

Marcy smiled and grabbed her son's hand. In a few minutes he'd be gone. She would not see him for a long time. Maybe forever.

"Son, I've done the best I could raising you. Just remember I love you. I'll always love you. You've been a wonderful son. Be careful. Be strong. Be safe…". Her lips quivered. She tried to say goodbye, but the words would not come.

He stood, hugged her for a minute or two, and walked out the door. Down the cinder block stairs of the trailer, and over to look at his car for the last time. Guess he'd never get to drive it now. Hoped his mom would save it for him.

The noise from his phone startled him. Buried deep in his backpack, he dug it out and looked to see who was calling him. *Samantha*. He couldn't answer it. From her, or from anybody.

He placed the phone on the front seat of the Chevy, disconnecting him from the GPS tracking system, his friends, his life. He had to have a clean break. He had to disappear.

So, he was leaving Dallas after all. But not in his tricked-out Chevy surrounded by friends. No sunny skies accented with white puffy clouds while he cruised down the highway listening to the radio.

This was not the kind of graduation he had envisioned. His high school diploma had been replaced by a hand-written map. His classic car by a five-year old bike purchased at a garage sale. His open highway would be an uncharted grassy path into the darkness of the Trinity Forest.

Post high school education awaited out in the streets of Dallas, or along the banks of the Trinity River, and beyond.

He looked down at his bike leaning against the trailer. It looked ready, eager to take him away. He got on and rode into the darkness.

PART TWO

PALEO

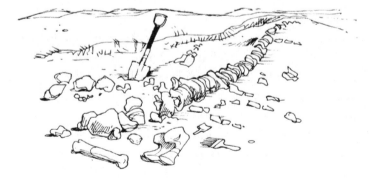

CHAPTER 19

It was a cool Wednesday morning in May when Salvador left the only home he'd ever known. He'd memorized the map Mr. T had given him, surprised that the path he sought was only a few miles away.

A hint of daylight appeared as he started his journey. Down San Augustine to highway 175 access road. From there he jumped on a dismantled dirt train track that led him to the sign he was searching for: *The Great Trinity Forest Way*.

So far, so good.

Traveling west toward the river he searched for the entrance into the forest that Mr. T had drawn on the map. Then he saw it: a four-foot wide entry between two tall oak trees. The tree on the left had a crumpled paper attached about three feet from the ground.

He guided his bike toward the path until he got close enough to read the small piece of paper attached to the tree, the marker he was looking for. E PLURIBUS UNUM, it read. He entered the trail.

The light from the morning instantly turned to darkness as he entered the forest. Tall trees and thick vines twisted in every direction. Shrubs and brush he'd never seen, though only a few miles from his home.

The temperature got cooler as the bike navigated the well-worn trail. His eyes strained to adjust to the shadows.

After about ten minutes the thick vegetation thinned out and light poured through the spaces in the canopy of the forest. A small opening appeared as he neared the banks of the river. He slowed his bike.

Soon he came upon an encampment of homeless people. Tents, broken down couches, rusted BBQ grills, and a big barrel with smoke billowing toward the sky. Trash was everywhere.

"Yo, what's up Holmes?"

It was a voice from behind. He stopped his bike and looked around. *Before he could see who was speaking a fist smashed against the side of his face, knocking him to the ground.*

He scrambled to his feet, looking in the direction of the voice and the attacker. "Get up punk!"

Sal shook his head to try to regain his senses and noticed three guys standing around him, grinning. His instincts kicked in. He charged head-first into the guy who was closest to him, knocking him to the ground. Sal started swinging but was stopped by a foot to his head from one of the attackers.

Then they were on top of him. Hands and legs pinned down, bashing his face. Laughing, cursing, and making fun of his attempts to fight back.

"You dumb-ass Mexican coming into my territory. I'm gonna mess you up bad Holmes. Jay Jay, make sure you get his money."

His attackers were about to continue the beating when a

loud commotion coming from the trail behind distracted their attention. They turned in unison to see what was happening.

"What the f...?"

A loud booming voice interrupted their words in mid-sentence.

CHAPTER 20

"WHOAAA! WHOAAA! WHOAAA! What's going on here?"

A middle-aged man riding a small vintage sting-ray bicycle rode up from behind and quickly dismounted, propelling the bike into the three predators.

The man was about 5'11". Weighed 190. Wore a Dallas Cowboys cap, a white t-shirt with CANCUN written on the front, army fatigues and combat boots. On his left arm a tattoo read 'JASMINE.'

U.S. Special Forces agent Ahmad, a Jordanian-born communications and combat specialist, was on a personal mission in Dallas that had nothing to do with the government.

He only had a few hours left before he returned home to his wife and daughter in Florida, then redeployed for his next combat assignment in Central America.

Ahmad had followed the leads he'd uncovered in Pensacola and they guided him to an apartment in Dallas, where he watched Salvador beat James Benson to within inches of his life. The same James Benson who'd been having sex with his 15-year old daughter on the beaches of Pensacola.

Ahmad owed Sal a debt of gratitude that Sal knew nothing about. He had begun to repay that debt by paying Salvador's bail. He would now continue to repay that debt.

Parking a rented van a very short distance from Sal's house, Ahmad watched Sal get on his bike and ride toward the Trinity River. He followed, guessing he might be of assistance.

The attackers pushed the small bike out of the way and started toward Ahmad. He swiftly backed up several steps and held his hands up.

"Wait a minute now, this guy your beating is a friend of mine. We're just riding through, on our way to downtown Dallas to meet some friends. We don't want trouble."

Sal's head throbbed as he lay on the wet grass. He sat up to see who was trying to protect him, and that's when the three predators walked toward the man, surrounding him.

One of the men began to speak: "Mr., you one DUMB motha...coming down here and gettin' in our business...that was a bad decision...now you got ta pay." And with that the man attacked.

How many times had he seen this? On the side streets of Bagdad. Along the border towns of Tanzania and the back alleys of Kandahar. Predators exploiting the perceived weakness of their fellow human beings. But they had misjudged this time.

Like lightning Ahmad thrust a powerful right cross into the face of the oncoming attacker, breaking his nose and causing a stream of blood to pour down his chin. A second later, a knee to the groin. The attacker bent over and took a double-fisted blow to the back of his neck. Out cold.

The other two rushed in together. Cat-like, Ahmad

dropped down on his haunches and came up with double elbows to their chins, exposing their midsection. He spun left with a foot to the groin and right with a heel to the other man's groin.

Bent over, he smashed his fist into each man's face and watched them fall to the ground.

A small crowd of the homeless had gathered around the scene. They were beginning to cheer Ahmad as he displayed his fighting skills against these scumbags that evidently had little popularity among their ranks.

Not yet finished, Ahmad quickly opened his backpack and retrieved several cords. He bound the hands and feet of each man that lay motionless on the ground.

One of the men came to life and started cursing and threatening the homeless watching the scene. Ahmed planted the bottom of his combat boot into the man's mouth, knocking out several teeth.

The small crowd erupted in applause and began to spit on the three men. Finally, they were seeing justice. Swift, raw street justice.

Ahmad dragged each of the three men several yards away and lay them across the main dirt pathway that crisscrossed the Great Trinity Forest in hopes that someone walking down the trail would alert the police.

Picking up his bike, Ahmad barked out a brief directive toward Sal. "We gotta roll bro." They hopped on their bikes and disappeared into the forest, headed toward downtown Dallas.

CHAPTER 21

Sal struggled to keep up with Ahmad as he led them down the worn river trail. The path narrowed and darkened, then opened up again. His body was beginning to feel better despite the beating he'd just taken.

They rolled slowly to a stop along the riverbank, next to a sandy opening with a few fallen tree logs jutting out into the water. A small boat, well cared for, was anchored along the shore. Ahmad cautiously surveyed the area. "Let's stop for a few minutes, get a quick game plan. That flat-bottom boat belongs to somebody. Stay alert."

Sal took a seat on a sawed-off tree trunk and spoke to Ahmad. "Thanks for saving me back there. I guess I need to pay more attention to what's going on. I was lucky you happened to come by."

Ahmad smiled and squatted a few feet from Sal. "It's no accident I came by. I followed you from your house this morning. I've been following you since last Saturday when you got arrested."

Sal looked confused. "Why you following me?"

Ahmad pulled a cigarette out of his backpack, fired it up and took a long drag. "Let's just say I work for the government. I take care of problems, bad people, bad situations. I can't tell you much more than that."

Ahmad took another drag of his cigarette and paced back and forth, looking for potential trouble that could pop instantly in their current environment.

Sal cleared his throat and looked directly at the special forces agent. "Sir, I want to thank you for saving my life. But I still don't understand. Why are you following me?"

CHAPTER 22

Ahmad smiled. "That's a good question. I'll answer that if you can tell me why you are runnin' from the law?"

Sal was momentarily taken back by the question, but quickly composed himself. "Last Saturday I almost killed a man who attacking my girlfriend. The police arrested me, and then somebody paid my bail to be relea…".

Sal stopped in mid-sentence. Suddenly it dawned on him. Could this be the man who paid his $100,000 bail? He looked at Ahmad quizzically.

"Yes, I paid your bail. You took care of a problem for me on Saturday. The man I was after was the man you nearly beat to death."

Ahmad continued, "I've got to leave Dallas in a few minutes. Should be enough time to get you ready."

"Ready for what?", Sal asked.

The trained and seasoned special forces agent looked at the young man with empathy. Sal had no idea about the dangerous world he had entered, mostly hidden from the law. A world where the rules are different, and the only goal, survival.

Ahmad walked quickly over to Sal and held out his hand. "Can I see what's in your backpack?" Sal hesitated, then handed him the pack. Ahmad rummaged through it, then tossed it back to Sal. "Your packs a little light, not smart for a guy who's on the run. Let's see if we can take care of that."

He reached into his own backpack and tossed several small clear plastic sacks of ready-made items to Sal: snacks, pocketknife, first aid kit, flashlight, and a few other items. "Here you go. Try to refill the food packets every few days."

Reaching into a side pocket, Ahmad grabbed a two-inch wide black strap with a zipper in the center. "Money belt. Holds money, important papers with names and numbers you don't want to lose. Goes on the inside of your pants. And here's your new drivers' license with your new name, new address, and new date of birth."

Sal took the new license and examined it. "*Barry Landry?* That's my new name?"

"Not bad, huh? It's a specialty of mine. Make sure you memorize the full name, address, dates, and everything else on the license in case you're being questioned by authorities."

Sal nodded and tried on his money belt. He put his new drivers' license in it, along with Mr. T's small map that had the name of the contact he could use for his escape from Dallas.

Suddenly, he remembered the thieves had taken his money. He double checked. *Gone! He began to panic. All of his money was gone!*

He looked up at Ahmad, who was displaying a small wad of cash for him to see. "Look'in for this? It's yours. I took it off the attackers when I was tying them up." Ahmad let out a big laugh.

Sal grinned. "Thanks. Hopefully, I'll get the hang of this." He put the cash in his money belt.

Ahmad grabbed his backpack, walked to the sandy opening along the river and sat cross-legged on the ground. "Sal, bring your pack and come on over. We need to run over a few things before I leave."

Sal picked up his pack, walked over to the beach area and sat down. He noticed Ahmad had his eyes closed and was breathing rhythmically.

Suddenly Ahmad opened his eyes. "Ready?"

CHAPTER 23

Ahmad had a brief flashback to the many initiation rituals that preceded each mission he had participated in around the world. Some included alcohol and tobacco. Others had food and chants and songs. Each was somber, as there was no guarantee of survival. He'd lost many friends in combat.

He listened to the gurgling of the river as it followed its course toward the Gulf of Mexico. Felt the warm afternoon wind drifting through the trees. Hopefully, his young friend would have the resilience to make it on the journey ahead of him.

"Sal, if you can follow just a few rules, your chances of survival are good." Ahmad spoke slowly, clearly, and with authority.

"The best muscle in your body is your mind. Be aware, keep your head on a swivel. Listen. Observe. Avoid dangerous situations and people. Learn to be guided by your instincts."

He continued. *"The best hand to hand combat technique is the one you don't use.* Only fight if you have to. Fights have dangerous, unpredictable outcomes, and should always be your last resort."

Ahmad took two bottles of water out of his pack and handed one to Sal. He then pulled out a cigarette and lit up. Sal watched as Ahmad took a long drag on his cigarette and blew the smoke slowly into the air. It rose and disappeared into the sky above.

Ahmad handed the cigarette to Sal. "Take a drag, but don't breathe it into your lungs. Just hold it in your mouth a few seconds and blow it into the air. Allow the burnt tobacco to rise into the heavens, a gift to the gods from the earth."

Sal took a hit on the cigarette and blew the smoke into the air.

"Now, let's go stand by the river." Ahmad rose, brushed the sand off his pants and walked over to within a foot of the water. Sal followed.

"Salvador, the river is always moving, continuously maneuvering through the land with a goal of emptying into the Gulf of Mexico. It follows one law, the law of gravity, which is a law of the universe."

He placed a hand on Sal's shoulder. "Learn from the river. When I leave keep moving, maneuver through the obstacles in front of you and keep your destination clear in your mind. Follow the laws of the universe."

And with that Ahmad gave Sal a handshake, jumped on his bike and rode back to the forest trail, disappearing into the trees.

The late afternoon sun peaked over the treetops on its way down. Sal looked around, watching the river flow on its south bound journey to the Gulf of Mexico. He listened to the strange sounds of the forest.

He was all alone.

Your mind. The strongest muscle in your body. Use your mind. Think.

Keep your head on a swivel. Act quickly. Keep moving.

He shook himself back into the reality of his situation. The police might soon find out he had left home and would be looking for him. He had to get out of the city.

He took out his money belt and pulled out the map Mr. T had given him. His contact was a short distance away on the edge of downtown, under a bridge. *PALEO. A strange name, but the man Mr. T trusted to take him safely away from the city of Dallas.*

Salvador jumped on his bike and followed the trail that led toward the skyscrapers of the city. His eyes were alert. His head swiveled back and forth, looking for danger that could come from any direction.

In minutes he was once again engulfed into the darkness of the forest.

CHAPTER 24

The vegetation thickened and the trail narrowed to about one foot in width, forcing Sal to get off his bike and walk it along the path. Erie sounds echoed off the branches of the trees. His muscles tensed, as every inch of his body sensed danger.

He smelt the smoke before he saw it, moving quickly to an opening just ahead. It was a familiar smell. A grill. Someone was cooking on a grill.

Salvador pushed his bike out of the forest trail and into an opening on the banks of the Trinity. He began to see glimpses of the tall skyscrapers of downtown Dallas. Sounds of cars driving on the interstate overhead got louder.

Emerging from the canopy of trees, Salvador saw two figures sitting at a folding table twenty feet away, engaged in conversation. Strange items lay on the table, which seemed to be the topic of conversation.

Sal rode cautiously toward the men, assessing the situation. One man was dressed in a grey suit, no tie, coat unbuttoned and dark curly hair. The other man had a wildness about him.

He was tanned, long-haired, and wore a thick leather strap around his neck with a large tooth attached.

He immediately identified the man on the right as the contact Mr. T had described on the map. Wild-looking, long grayish-brown hair pulled back into a ponytail, hiking boots.

The two men stopped their conversation as Sal approached on his bike. The tall, tanned man stood and faced Sal cautiously.

"Entry code?"

Sal cleared his throat. *"E Pluribus Unum."*

Paleo flashed a big smile and nodded. "Salvador! Mr. T said you might show up soon. Looks like you made it in time for dinner. Chen's about to take the vegetables off the grill."

Sal looked at the man who was speaking to him.

"PALEO. The name's Paleo. Welcome to La Reunion. Want a beer?" Paleo reached into his cooler, pulled out a Corona and handed it to Sal.

Sal rarely drank, but he knew this was a gesture of friendship. He opened it and took a long swallow. The ice-cold beer tasted good. "Thanks, much appreciated."

"We only drink Mexican beer down here. Corona, Dos Equis, Pacifico. Ain't that right judge?"

The man in the suit looked up and hoisted his beer toward Sal.

"Cold...Mexican beer. Here's to America. Here's to La Reunion."

"What's that mean?", Sal asked.

"La Reunion? It was the name of a French Utopian Colony that came to Dallas in 1855. They built a settlement just a few miles down the river from where we're camped. Tried to install socialism in America, right here in Texas. The colony only lasted a few years, then fell apart. I guess they didn't know

America was founded on capitalism. Bunch of dumb sumbitches."

Paleo bent down and tied one of his boots. "But the difference between their settlement and my campsite is that WE believe in being rewarded for hard work. No entitlement bullshit down here, and no freebies! Get off your ass and work. We buy, sell, and trade. It's how we survive."

The judge reached over to the middle of the newspaper-covered folding table and placed several of the strange specimens in a pile. Standing up from the wood stump that served as a chair, he walked toward Paleo.

"Paleo, this is my final offer. $900 for the three mammoth teeth, two camel tibias, and the Mesosaurus vertebrae. Take it or leave it. I've got to get home and clean up for a fundraiser tonight."

Paleo smiled. "Well, now you're talk'in my language. Top me off at $1,000 and you got a deal. I'll have them all wrapped up for you when you come back in the morning. You can slap the lettuce on me then."

The judge shook hands with Paleo and headed back in the direction of downtown Dallas along a dirt path.

"Customer of mine. We've done business together for about ten years. He's been a collector of dinosaur bones for decades, specializing in mammoth and mastodons."

Paleo pointed toward the Judge as he disappeared in the distance. "Interesting fellow. Came up from Central America as an orphaned boy in the '70's after his parents were killed in a civil war. Adopted by an old white couple in Granbury. Loves America for taking him in. Giving him a home, and opportunity."

Paleo looked at Sal and noticed the scratches on his face and arms, and the swelling on the side of his head. "Have a seat Sal. Let's talk a few minutes while we finish our beer. Looks like you had a little action on the way here."

Sal sat down on the stump the judge had occupied. He was exhausted. He took off his backpack, laid it on the table, and took a deep breath.

For the next five minutes he told Paleo about his morning and afternoon encounters. Paleo listened attentively and was about to respond when two young drifters veered towards Paleo's area.

"Hey man, got a beer?" The tone of the man's request was rude.

CHAPTER 25

Paleo stepped out into the open, looking the two over. He didn't recognize them but was familiar with their type. Cocky young white skinheads with swastika's exposed. Tattoo's and piercings everywhere.

They were fidgety and seemed restless. *He sensed trouble.*

Paleo smiled. "Sorry gentleman, we only have enough for our dinner tonight."

Chen appeared out of nowhere and positioned himself beside Paleo. Though only 5' 2" and 130 pounds, Chen was well-traveled. Scars of all shapes and sizes covered his body, a warning to a more cautious breed of a man to think twice about throwing down a challenge.

"That's bullshit man! We saw you pull a cold beer out of that big cooler when we were walking by."

One of the drifters mumbled disgustedly and walked over to the cooler. "We don't play that game old man! I need a cold one!" The tattooed degenerate bent over, opened the top of the cooler, and was reaching in when the lid slammed violently against his fingers.

"Ahhhhhh! You broke my hand dammit."

Sal watched spellbound. Chen had moved swiftly and jumped on top of the cooler as the drifter was helping himself to a beer.

"Like my friend said, we're running a little low on beer tonight, so why don't you walk right down that dirt path over there to the liquor store. Lots of cold beer there." Chen pointed toward the trail.

"You little piece of shit...I'll kick your ass!" The drifter grabbed at Chens leg but was too late. Chen had sprung into the air and extended his right foot into the face of the intruder. His head snapped back violently as it whiplashed from the blow. He lay sprawled out on the ground.

Paleo pulled out a one-foot razor sharp machete that hung on a scabbard on the right side of his waist and walked to within inches of the second intruder. Wild-eyed, he laid the blade gently on the drifter's cheek, applying pressure 'til blood trickled down his quivering chin.

"Pick up your friend and get your sorry asses out of here. Don't come back until you learn how to respect a man's property."

The man's face had turned from arrogance to shock. He was trembling as he picked up his friend and dragged him away.

Chen and Paleo watched for several minutes until the men were far down the path.

Paleo slapped Sal on the back. "Come on Sal, time to eat. Chen's specialty awaits."

CHAPTER 26

Chen moved briskly as he prepared dinner. He picked up a sack of paper plates and plastic utensils in a box by the cooler, and methodically set the table.

"Time to eat boys."

Paleo packed his merchandise that lay on their dinner table and took it over to his small tent by the edge of the forest. When he arrived back, Chen had everything ready: grilled vegetables, pork and beans, and rice. The smell was tantalizing.

As the three sat for dinner, Paleo grabbed his beer and lifted it high into the air: "Here's to our guest, SALVADOR." Each took a drink, and the meal began.

"We", pointing at Chen, "have the master chef. Chen can cook anything and make it taste good, even an alligator turd."

Chen smiled. "That's one of my specialties. I just use a little extra seasoning."

Two policemen rode by on mountain bikes. "Afternoon Paleo. Chen." Paleo greeted the policemen. Sal froze in fear but nodded toward the officers, uncertain if they were already looking for him.

Chen rose quickly. "Good evening officers." He was about to reseat himself when a young boy ran up to their camp, out of breath.

"Mr. Chen! Mr. Chen! You promised we could fish today. Mom let me leave the shelter to come here, but I have to be back before six."

Chen smiled and nodded to the young man. "Well Johnny, we got about an hour before it gets dark. Let's go try our luck." They watched as the boy and Chen strolled down to the river.

Paleo had noticed how Sal tensed up when the police rode by. "Know why the police didn't stop and question us, or you?" He didn't wait for an answer. "It's because they know Chen and I don't break the law. They've watched us for years. We BEND it a little bit, but we don't break it."

Sal nodded. "I didn't know if they were looking for me yet, so I was about to pull out that new fake drivers' license I got and hand it to the officer."

Paleo smiled. "Well, looks like you're in the same boat as the rest us. Most people down here are either runnin' from the law or hiding out for one reason or another, using fake names or nicknames they've made up. Including me and Chen."

Sal stared at Paleo, bewildered. *Who is this guy?*

CHAPTER 27

"Yep. Paleo's my nickname. It's all I go by. Had it before I started my business in Dallas. Chen made his name up years ago when he first arrived from New Orleans."

Paleo noticed Sal listening with rapt attention. He loved holding court.

"Chen grew up in a small town on the Mekong Delta in Vietnam. Got a job on a river boat at 13 and left home. He was soon captaining that boat 'til he joined the war."

Paleo opened the cigar box and picked one out. "Told me the war affected him, so he decided to hop on an ocean liner and drift around a little bit. Indonesia. Australia. Europe. He drifted for years." Paleo stood and looked around.

"Finally landed in South America and got a job he really liked on the Amazon River, guiding for adventure seekers from around the world. Met a girl from New Orleans who was on a week-long trip, fell in love, and moved down to the bayou to be with her. They stayed together for about a year. She came home late one night and was raped and killed."

Paleo swatted away a large bug that had landed on his

shoulder. "It took him a month, but Chen found out who did it and dispensed justice. Some local fishermen in New Orleans found the lifeless body of that man on the bottom of the Mississippi River. At that point Chen decided to start a new life in Dallas."

Sal was entranced. "Does he live down here all year long?"

"Naw. Splits his time between here and the Austin Street Shelter, where he works as a cook. He's been cooking and practicing martial arts since he was 13. Expert at both."

Sal was on the edge of his tree stump, engrossed in the story.

"How did you get down here, Paleo? And how do you know Mr. T?"

CHAPTER 28

Paleo nodded toward Sal. He cleared the table of the food and the used newspapers that served as a tablecloth. Grabbed a roll of paper towels and some cleaner and meticulously wiped off the table.

"We make sure our campsite is squeaky clean. Keeps the animals, birds and insects away. And the police."

Paleo reached for the cigar box. Got one for himself and handed one to Sal.

"T and I were freshman together at University of New Mexico in Albuquerque, majoring in archeology. We were both fascinated with ancient cultures, ruins, and dinosaurs. Early on we were going on excavation trips with the school."

Paleo smiled whimsically. "Within a few years we'd learned the basics of archaeology in the southwest, and by the time I was a senior we were skipping classes for weeks at a time. That was until the department chair called us into his office. Said he was going to kick us out of the program unless we got serious about school."

"'TO HELL WITH IT!'" That's what I told him. I got up

and walked out. Never returned. It was an easy decision for me, but not for Mr. T. He'd promised his mom from the time he was twelve that he'd get a master's degree in history and archaeology and become a teacher. And that's what he did."

Darkness was beginning to blanket the landscape around the small campsite. Chen walked up, reached into the cooler, and pulled out a bottle of water. "See you guys in the morning." He disappeared in the direction of the forest.

Paleo dug a portable lamp out of his tent and placed it on the table. "Long day tomorrow Sal, so we better hit the sack. Your bike will be safe here by the table but keep your backpack by your side at all times." He rolled the bike to the table and leaned it against one of the tree stumps.

"There's your tent. I got your sleeping bag ready."

Sal entered the tent, sprawled out on top of his sleeping bag fully clothed, and was soon asleep.

CHAPTER 29

Sounds of the birds in the forest took over the quietness of the night, and Sal opened his eyes. The soft morning light offered some opportunity to look around. *Where was he? A tent. He was sleeping in a tent at Paleo's campsite on the Trinity River.*

He located his backpack in the corner, picked it up and dug around to make sure everything was there.

What was that around his waist? He reached down to find the money belt on the inside of his pants. He examined the contents and found the notes from Mr. T and Troy, some money, and a drivers' license with his new name: Barry Landry.

And then anxiety flooded his body. *He had to get out of Dallas and away from the police who might soon be looking for him.*

He heard voices outside and exited the tent. Looking around, he noticed several homeless men walking along a dirt path, only feet from the river that would take him out of the city.

Paleo sat at the table with a young college-aged male, looking through the pages of a book. Sal walked over and noticed both were drinking coffee and looking at pictures of dinosaurs in a college textbook.

"Mornin' Sal. Komodo Dragon's on the camp stove. Extra coffee cup in the cooler. Help yourself. We'll head out in a little bit." Sal poured himself a cup and walked back to where Paleo and the student were engaged in a discussion.

"The Dallasaurus Turneri specimen was found by a construction worker north of here in the late 1980's. It lived in the shallow seas when this area was underwater ninety million years ago. The guy that found it took the specimen to the Dallas Museum of Natural History to find out what it was. Created quite a stir."

The young man looked at Paleo, confused: "But my professor said that...."

"Your professor don't know SHIT! He needs to get off the computer and get his ass down here in the sand and the water to find out what the hell is going on."

Paleo shook his head in disbelief. He looked intently at the young man.

"You telling me he never takes his students out to McCommas Bluffs, or the Trinity Terrace sand deposits? How about the Archosaur Site in North Arlington that's being excavated by UTA?"

Sal sipped the bitter dark coffee, fascinated with the conversation underway in the shadows of the city. He took a seat at the table, noticing the faded painting on top: *Corona*.

"Listen Preston, I've only got a few minutes before I have to go to Fort Worth. Here's a list of a few places in Texas you need to visit and become knowledgeable about if you want to work with me as an intern next year."

Paleo handed him a pen and a notepad. "Write these down: Big Bend, Paluxy River, Archosaur Site, Waco

Mammoth Pit, and the Panhandle-Plains History Museum in Canyon. Don't come back until you visit and study these sites, then we'll talk."

Preston shook Paleo's hand, picked up his college textbook and headed back toward the city of Dallas.

Paleo watched as the young man left. "Nice kid. He heard about me from a former intern of mine during a paleontology conference in Wyoming a few weeks ago."

Paleo stood, walked over to the coffee pot and poured himself a cup. "Sal, want another shot of gusto?" Sal walked over and Paleo topped him off.

"That college boy asked me what the secret is to finding dinosaur bones." Paleo casually looked around the campsite.

"So, what is the secret to finding dinosaur bones, Paleo?"

Paleo grabbed a cigar off the table and lit up. "If I tell you it won't be a secret anymore Sal, will it." He took a long drag on the cigar. "Tell you what, when we get to Fort Worth later today, you can ask Leroy, my director of operations there. See if he wants to let you in on it."

CHAPTER 30

Chen walked quickly up to Paleo, body drenched in sweat.

"Boats ready boss. Gas full, boxes loaded. Can't take Sal's bike to Ft. Worth, not enough room. When you guys head'in out?"

"Five minutes. I've got to stop in Arlington for about an hour to close on a business deal with one of my clients, so we might not get to Fort Worth 'til late this afternoon. I'll be back Tuesday unless something comes up."

Paleo took a seat at the table by Salvador.

"Sal, we need to take care of a little business before we head to Fort Worth. It's about your bike. You can't take it on the boat, so I'll buy it from you. Most I can pay is $100. That's top wholesale price, and about what I can sell it for at the flea market."

"But, since you will probably be staying at my riverfront condo in Fort Worth for the next three nights, you'll be paying me $25 per night, for a total of $75. That leaves you $25." Paleo laid a twenty and a five on the table. "Here you go, take it or leave it."

Sal was unaccustomed to making deals in the marketplace, but he trusted Paleo and picked up the money.

"I'll take it. Thanks Paleo."

"No problem. The dinner and the room last night were courtesy of your friendship with Mr. T. Same with the boat ride to Fort Worth. After that you pay like everybody else. Welcome to the real world. No entitlement bullshit down here, and no freebies. This ain't the U.S. Congress." Paleo grinned. "I don't need your vote."

PART THREE

COW TOWN

CHAPTER 31

The small metal boat idled lazily on the banks of the Trinity, waiting for its two travelers. Once they climbed in, Paleo positioned himself on a wooden plank, grabbed an oar and maneuvered the tiny craft into the flow of the current.

Thus propelled by the river's natural movement, he dropped the oar and placed his hand on the throttle of the Evinrude motor, guiding them down the brown muddy river as it snaked back and forth across the land.

Salvador sat up front, glancing at the variety of broken twigs, limbs and logs floating in the water. Over to his left he saw a long straight branch moving up beside the boat. *Suddenly the branch splashed and moved quickly toward the shore.*

"Look! What's that?"

Paleo glanced down nonchalantly. "Alligator Gar, six-footer. Trace their ancestors back to the late Jurassic Period, about 150 million years ago. A guy caught one a few years ago that was over three-hundred pounds."

Sal felt his senses come alive as they cruised down the Trinity. Past tall trees, industrial buildings and houses. They crossed underneath a few bridges and meandered through the ancient waterway as people had done for centuries.

He turned around and noticed Paleo looking for something on the right side of the bank. "There it is Sal, our first stop. I've got to meet one of my clients here. We'll have lunch, complete the transaction and roll down the river to cow town."

Paleo drove the boat slowly onto the bank next to a large tree. He nimbly jumped out and secured the craft.

"Sal, be careful when you get out. There's a big water moccasin three feet in front of the boat." Sal watched the snake slither off the bank and into the water.

After about a five-minute walk they approached a beautifully manicured patch of grass that stretched into the distance toward a building. Two men in shorts rode up to them on a golf cart.

"Well, look who showed up, '*Trump on the Trinity*'! What took you so long Paleo, you dino-huntin' sumbitch. Thought you'd be here at tee time and have a little breakfast with us. We're already on the 16th hole."

Paleo walked up to the golf cart and extended his hand.

"Sorry Jim. Had to take care of a little business for a close friend of mine, so it pushed me back a few hours. But I sure would like to play the last three holes with you guys so I can win some of that rich folk money."

The golfers both laughed, and one reached into their cooler.

"Corona?" He handed Sal and Paleo a cold beer.

"Thanks Jim. If you don't mind could we drop off my friend at the clubhouse so he can get some lunch? Then we'll finish the last three holes and head back to the clubhouse. I'll show you those new specimens I got last week from a collector in McKinney."

Sal and Paleo climbed onto the back seat of the large golf cart and headed over to the clubhouse restaurant. "Sal, go ahead and get you something to eat. We'll be back in a little bit."

Sal jumped off the golf cart, walked into the clubhouse and found a seat at a table by the window. The waitress approached.

"Morning sir, can I take your order?"

"Yes mam. I'll take a cheeseburger and a coke."

As the waitress walked away, Salvador reached into his money belt and pulled out his new drivers' license. He examined it closely, reading every word.

Name, Barry Landry. Age, 17. Height, 6'0". Weight, 160 lbs. Eyes, brown. Hair, black. Address, 5617 Patagonia Way, etc.... He read it again before putting it back into his money belt.

CHAPTER 32

After paying his bill, Sal looked out of the window of the clubhouse restaurant and saw Paleo and the two golfers sitting on the patio, a small stack of cash piled in the middle of their table. He walked out to join them. One of the golfers shoved the money over to Paleo in disgust.

"Birdie, birdie, eagle, with a 300-yard drive on the 18th hole! How in the HELL does a homeless sumbitch livin' under a bridge in Dallas drive the ball that far without practice?"

Paleo grinned as he scooped up his winnings. "Thanks for the donation boys. Now, let's get down to business."

Reaching into his shouldered canvas bag, Paleo pulled out the contents and spread them out on the table. The golfers reached out, picked up several specimens and examined them admiringly.

"Hate to say it Paleo, but these Megalodon teeth are awesome. My grandkids will love 'em. Tell you what, I'll trade ten of your best specimens here for two primo Dallas Cowboys tickets."

Paleo took a moment to consider the offer. "Who are the

'Boys playing?"

The golfer pulled out an envelope from his golf bag and tossed the tickets on the table. "Cowboys-Eagles home game. Front row seats on the fifty-yard line. Hate to miss it, but I'll be down in Midland closing on an oil deal. Most people don't think the Cowboys got a chance."

"Thanks Jim. I believe I'll take that trade. Hard to say who'll win the game, since it's a big NFC East rivalry."

Paleo and Sal headed back to the river. As they approached the boat, Paleo scanned the banks. "All clear Salvador. Jump in and I'll push us off."

The air was thick with humidity and the sun became intense as the small metal craft cruised down the Trinity. In the distance clouds were beginning to form.

This was the time of the year when strong thunderstorms and tornados could pop up quickly. Winds from the south carried moisture from the Gulf of Mexico and collided with the dry winds from the north.

Conditioned through decades of living outside, Paleo surveyed the sky. "We've got to watch out for the weather for the next several days. May get a little rain in the afternoons or even a bad storm."

The boat moved slowly through the water and time dragged by at a snail's pace. Paleo noticed Sal getting restless. "Sal, ever fished the Trinity River?"

Sal shook his head no.

"If you would like to give it a try, there's a Zebco under your seat. Its' even got the lure on it, so all you have to do is cast out. Helps pass the time on this stretch of the trip. And, you never know what you'll catch."

Sal grabbed the rod, pressed the release button and tossed it out. The lure traveled only two feet before plopping into the water. Paleo laughed loudly.

"Good thing we got some time. Go ahead and practice your casting. Try to get it out about twenty feet from the boat. While you're practicing, just remember that the power is in the arm, but the accuracy is in the wrist."

Five minutes went by, then ten. Sal practiced his casting and soon was placing the lure out about twenty feet.

"Damn you learn quick," Paleo belted out.

As soon as he said it Sal felt a strong jerk on his rod which nearly came out of his hands. He pulled up tightly, feeling the strength of the fish on the other end.

"Hang on Sal! Could be a big one." Sal tightened his grip as the rod bent double. "I'll slow the boat down."

Paleo put the motor in low gear and eased the boat in the direction of the line. Sal was struggling with the fish, unable to bring it up. They got closer to where the line entered the water, and something roiled just beneath the murky surface.

"Not sure what that is you caught. Let me pull it up." Paleo grabbed a long wood stick with a metal hook on the end and placed it in the water, trying to latch on to the fish. He felt something attach and pulled it forcefully to the surface. "What the hell is that?"

CHAPTER 33

Paleo handed the pole to Sal. "Hold this Sal while I take this THING off the hook." Plyers in hand, Paleo twisted it back and forth several times until it loosened and dropped into the boat, making a CLINK sound. Finally, he pulled off the wet vegetation that covered the item and brushed the mud away.

"I'll be damned! Looks like an old rifle of some kind. We'll clean it up when we get into Fort Worth and show it to a few antique dealers. If my youngest son was here, he'd be able to tell us what we got."

"Didn't know you had a son Paleo. Where does he live?"

"Depends of the time of the year. Right now, he's up in Montana on the Hell Creek Formation, hunting dinosaur bones with some ranchers. Lives in a small beat-up travel trailer."

"In a few months he'll drag the trailer down to Moab, Utah, where he takes people on rafting trips on the Green River. When he's not on the river he's out looking for Jurassic specimens. He'll stay in Moab till October or November when it starts getting cold."

Paleo dug into one of the pockets of his fisherman's vest and pulled out a cigar. He took his time as he lit it, looking around at the river surroundings.

"Then it's on to Quartzite, Arizona, where we meet up and work the flea markets and the rock shows of Arizona during the winter, November to March. Lots of snowbirds and drifters spend the winter there. I own a few acres and a small trailer."

Sal nodded, "So he's takin' after the old man."

"Yea. He's eat up with dinosaurs and driftin'. But my youngest son is the exact opposite. He's a 'Suit' making six figures in the Silicon Valley. Nice house, expensive cars, exotic vacations. In debt up to his ass-hole."

The river veered left as they approached a major freeway packed with cars. Close by, the skyline of Fort Worth was silhouetted against white clouds and a blue sky.

"Getting close. The river-front condo is right around the bend."

Soon an old railroad bridge appeared. Just this side of the bridge Sal could see the figure of a man in motion on the banks of the river.

"Looks like Leroy's doing his training for the day. Same workout routine as Hershel Walker, his favorite Dallas Cowboy legend. 1,000 pushups, 1,500 sit-ups." Paleo guided the boat in the direction of the bank. "Hey Leroy!", he shouted. "Is it dinner time yet?"

"Taco Thursday Paleo! Rick starts serving at 4, so we got about thirty minutes to unload and walk over to the food truck. He sold out last week by five o'clock."

The boat slid onto the bank and Paleo tossed the rope to Leroy. Leroy caught the rope in mid-air and secured it to a large cottonwood tree. An 8' x 10' tent sat close by, next to an American flag.

Leroy's physical presence radiated strength. He stood 6-foot tall and wore a short-sleeve Dallas Cowboy jersey, exposing his chiseled forearms. Muscular carved quadriceps bulged from his shorts, adding to a physique that revealed the slender waist and hips of a born athlete. He moved with quickness and ease.

"What's that you got here boss?" Leroy picked up the rifle Sal caught in the river and examined it thoroughly. "Looks like an old Remington or Winchester. Lots of dealers will be interested in this."

"Sal, this is my Fort Worth Division manager of business operations on the Trinity, Leroy. Leroy, this is Salvador, a friend of a very close friend of mine. He'll be working with us for a few days."

Leroy reached out his oversized hand toward Sal.

"Welcome brother Salvador. Glad to have you with us. Hope you're hungry cause Rick don't play when it comes to serving tacos!"

The three walked up the dirt trail that led to the top of the bridge. From there, they took the narrow wood path on the bridge that led across the Trinity. Paleo stretched his neck, looking toward the west. "I just saw the food truck pull up. We better hurry."

They approached the truck and were the first in line. The smell of seasoned ground taco meat filled the air.

"Buenos tardes, amigos. Que gustaria comer?" Rick smiled at the three men.

"Hola Rick. Buenos tardes. Nuevo tacos, por favor. And tres Coca-cola. Quanto questo?"

"Twenty-five bucks Paleo. How's business?"

"Not bad. Got some new merchandise you might want to look at."

"You already got half my paycheck from last month." Rick grinned and continued fixing their order.

"Always good karma to invest with the 'ole man'." Paleo dropped three ten-dollar bills on the window ledge. "Keep the change amigo."

Rick smiled and placed the sack full of tacos on the take-out counter. "Here you go my friend. I'll try to swing by Sunday, see what you got."

Paleo picked up their order and led the trio to a broken slab of concrete on the east side of Henderson Avenue, close to the railroad tracks.

Perched on their concrete dining table, Leroy noticed a gathering of clouds toward the southwest. "Paleo, winds pickin' up and the sky's lookin' dark green and black. Could be a bad storm coming our way."

CHAPTER 34

Paleo took a bite of his taco, watching the menacing thunderheads hover above the city. Without warning swirls of dust filled the air, and people scurried into their cars to escape the approaching storm.

Lightening flashed and thunder cracked loudly, followed by strong gusts of wind. And then the rain hit. "Let's get out of here!" yelled Paleo, running toward the gate at the back of the Henderson Market.

The rain turned to hail as Paleo jumped through an opening in the fence, followed by Leroy and Sal. The small round ice struck against their flesh like bullets, sending waves of pain through their bodies.

In the fury of the sudden storm, Leroy pulled out a set of keys and unlocked the padlock on the back of a large step-side cargo van. He lifted the bar on the door and opened the back to allow Sal and Paleo to jump in.

The door flew violently open. Leroy grabbed it, and with all his strength pulled the door shut as he jumped in. Though soaking wet and pelted with hail stones, they had made it safely into the van.

The crash of rain and hail against the sides of the van echoed loudly. Winds howled, rocking the van back and forth. Sirens continued their loud warning to take cover. Any cover.

Time seemed to drag on during the initial burst of the storm. And then the intensity eased. The hail stopped and rain fell in a gentle pitter-patter.

Paleo rose from the floor of the van and flipped on a light. Sal looked around, mesmerized. Paintings, beautiful and unusual, covered the walls. Antiques and books were stacked neatly on shelfs in the back of the van, along with many small boxes, each with a series of names, numbers and codes.

A small cot for sleeping sat on one side of the van, accompanied by a nightstand and a small lamp. Several books lay close by.

"What'd ya think of our Fort Worth storage facility Sal?", Paleo asked.

"Love the paintings." Sal walked closer to the get a better view.

Leroy walked over to Sal, pointing to the signature on the bottom. "This one is by a self-taught Texas artist, Ran Horn. He's been featured in Texas Monthly." They admired the work of this former preacher-turned-painter.

Sal moved to the next painting, Leroy right behind.

"That's a Shonto Begay piece, a well-known Navajo painter. He's got a style similar to Van Gogh and Ran Horn, called BROKEN STOKE. Took me awhile to close the deal on the Begay painting. I had to give the guy a pair of Lucchese ostrich boots, one small uncut emerald, and $500 cash."

Paleo unbolted the metal bar on the inside of the van and pushed open the door. A cool rush of wind greeted them.

Leroy jumped down on the asphalt parking lot, took his

shirt off and reached both arms toward the sky. A light, gently falling rain cooled his muscular body. "Ahhhhhhh! Didn't know I was sweating so much in there."

Sal noticed the massive layered muscles on Leroy's body, and the tiny bullet ridden scars on his chest where a bronze medallion lay.

"Leroy, what's that medal you're wearing?", asked Sal.

Leroy looked down at the medal on his body.

"Ah, it's just something they gave me when I got injured in Iraq five years ago. I didn't do much, but I like wearin' it cause I love my country. My father and my grandfather also fought in the military. Vietnam and Korea."

Paleo began to walk the premises, looking at the debris left behind from the storm. He noticed that the damage wasn't too bad. Just a few cracked windshields from the hail and a lot of branches and leaves from the trees.

"We got lucky, no tornados. Let's go check out our tent across the river."

They quickly crossed the bridge and were standing in front of the riverside tent, inspecting the aftermath of the storm. "Amazing! Still standing." Paleo looked at Leroy in disbelief. "How did you secure this tent to handle a storm like that?"

Leroy grinned. "Just a few tricks they taught us in the military during survival training. And a little luck."

Paleo opened the flap and stepped inside, picking up several items he had brought with them on the boat from Dallas.

"Let's take the rest of the merchandise in the tent and load up the El Camino. Clint called me when I was on the golf course and said we need to be at Traders Village tonight. He's got something he wants me to see. Said he had a big trade in the works."

Paleo continued. "Sal, don't forget to get your rifle. There're a few old traders who will be able to identify it. Might be worth something."

CHAPTER 35

Sal woke in the early morning hours and looked around the room. It was a small bedroom, if you could call it that. A tiny kitchen was just a few feet away, and beyond that was Leroy, sleeping on the couch.

There was a knock on the door. "Breakfast time boys. We'll leave in fifteen minutes for the Waffle House."

They both dressed, maneuvering around each other in the close confines of the small trailer. Leroy led Sal through the RV parking lot of Traders Village, passing a swimming pool and several travel trailers 'til they reached Clint's truck.

Clint eased out of Traders Village and in no time found himself pulling into the last parking spot at the Waffle House.

"Table for four?" They nodded, and the waitress seated them. Sal scanned the room, closely watching the movement of the waitresses, thinking about his mom.

"Clint, this is Salvador. He'll be working with me and Leroy at Traders' Village tomorrow, then helping us on Sunday at the Henderson Bazaar."

Clint was a tall, slow-moving Texan whose words were

measured for maximum impact. He smiled and reached out his hand toward Sal. "Glad to meet you Salvador. Hope you and Leroy slept alright in the Casita. I leave it at the Village year-round for dealer friends to use when they come to town for the market."

The waitress arrived with coffee and placed her empty hand on her hip. She stared at Paleo, a small grin on her face. "Ain't seen you in a while Paleo. Thought you got eaten by one of them big dinosaurs you dug up." She pinched him on the check and winked.

"Nothin' could keep me from you darlin', not even a T-Rex."

She rolled her eyes and shook her head as she walked away, Paleo's eyes following the contours of her body.

Clint laughed loudly. "When you gonna grow up and settle down Paleo?"

"Overrated. A man needs room to move around, room to breathe."

Clint chuckled and continued.

"Last month I was down at the Warrenton Antique Show, hanging out with a dealer friend of mine. He asked me if I wanted to buy his entire collection. Said he was going through a divorce and it was costing him a fortune. I hesitated, but then he threw out a number I couldn't refuse. The merchandise will be delivered today."

"Clint, what type of inventory did you get?" Leroy asked.

"Couple of old motorcycles, antique guns, and lots of vintage Native American jewelry. There're also some Navajo rugs, five western paintings, and about thirty heavy cardboard boxes of miscellaneous stuff that hadn't been opened in twenty years. No telling what we'll find in them boxes."

Clint took a sip of coffee. "Paleo, if you don't mind, I sure would appreciate you boys giving me a hand with unloading. And, there's a lot of pieces that I don't know the value of. Maybe you and Leroy can pitch in your two cents on those."

Breakfast arrived and the discussion was put on hold. They devoured the food and sat, savoring their coffee.

Paleo pulled out a pair of worn dice from his vest pocket and rubbed them together. "Clint, ready to try your luck? Low-roll pays for breakfast."

"Let em fly!"

Paleo let the dice roll gently from his hand. "A six and a five. ELEVEN! Show me what you got Clint!"

Clint picked up the dice and shook them for several seconds before tossing them on the table.

"A six...and a six. Twelve! Get your money out son. Gonna be a good weekend."

The day flew by quickly as the men busied themselves with unloading, pricing, and separating items for the sale on Saturday. Sal noticed that Leroy's advice was always considered during the final identification and pricing.

At the end of the day, Sal lay stretched out on his tiny bed, exhausted. He was surprised at the amount of work required to sell at a flea market and amazed at the vast knowledge of the antique dealers.

Just as he was about to surrender to sleep, his mind drifted to the bloody scene of the man he'd nearly beaten to death. Anxiety shot through his body and he sprang up in bed.

Did the man from Florida die? Have the police found out he left Dallas? Sal tossed and turned for hours before finally falling asleep.

CHAPTER 36

Saturday came early, and with it an air of excitement at Traders Village. Golf carts and bikes moved across the asphalt pathways carrying dealers and merchandise. Storage facilities were being emptied and placed on tables for sale.

Cars, trucks, vans and vehicles of every kind were parking at their designated spots, displaying merchandise for sale. Entire families were setting up tents, eating breakfast and visiting with fellow traders. There was movement everywhere, and the energy was electric.

Paleo walked up to space #1888, a corner lot next to the Northeast entrance, carrying three coffees and a bag of sausage-biscuits from McDonalds. Sal was there with Leroy, setting up their 10' x12' space.

"Leroy, that Dallas Cowboy dealer stopped me on the way to McDonald's. Wanted me to tell you that he found a signed Bullet Bob Hayes jersey."

Dropping the box he was holding, Leroy's hand flashed toward the sack of biscuits. Pulling several out, he grabbed his coffee and sprinted away.

Paleo laughed. "Leroy loves three things: God, America, and the Dallas Cowboys."

Sal opened his sausage-biscuit and squeezed out two packets of mustard. "How'd Leroy start working with you Paleo?"

Paleo put his coffee on the merchandise table and pulled out a Monte Cristo from his fishing vest.

"About five years ago Chen and I were pickin' the Henderson market on a Sunday morning. I guess that was about six months after Leroy had been honorably discharged from the army and awarded the purple heart."

"We heard a commotion and looked toward the railroad tracks. Four drifters were roughing up an old homeless man, digging through his bags and his bedroll. We went to help, but Leroy was already there."

Leaning against their merchandise table, Paleo fired up his unlit cigar and took a puff. "Next thing we saw was Leroy, all fist and elbows and feet, flying into the bodies of the attackers. Laid em out cold."

"Then we watched as Leroy put his hands on that old man's forehead, prayed for him, and gave him some cash. After that he walked over to the four men he'd just beat up, placed small new testaments into their pockets, and prayed for them too."

Paleo smiled as he reminisced. "Well, we invited him to lunch and found out he was camped out on the river. Also found out that he not only loved antiques but was incredibly knowledgeable about them. Learned it from his mom."

"Did he ever say why he was living on the river?"

Paleo nodded. "Said the war made his mind restless, and that God told him to live with the homeless for a while to help heal his mind. I offered him a job on the spot, and he's been with us ever since."

Clint drove up in his golf cart with Leroy in the passenger seat, wearing a vintage Bullet Bob Hayes jersey and a grin the size of Texas. Clint was wearing a long-sleeve western shirt. Around his neck was a massive silver bolo with two rough-cut blue turquoise stones, accented by a snake design.

"Morning Paleo. I dug out the two boxes of rough turquoise in storage for your friend that's coming through. Only got about fifty dollars in each box, so you can cut whatever deal you want. The boxes are sitting here on the back of the cart. What time did you say he'd be here?"

"Sometime this morning. He's traveling through on a slow drift back to his home on the Navajo reservation. Stayed with my friend Mr. T last night in Dallas and asked if I had any inventory. Sal, can you put those two boxes on the table?"

Sal walked over and picked up the boxes of turquoise, placing them gently on the display table.

From around the corner an old man with a long grey ponytail approached the table. He had dark brown skin and deep-set eyes. Wore jeans, a large rodeo belt buckle, and a black t-shirt.

Sal noticed a bracelet on his left arm, similar in style to the one Samantha had given him. In his right hand he held a cup of coffee.

"Ya 'at 'eeh. Hello my friend, Paleo. It's been a few years." The old man's words were spoken with a gentle-staccato accent.

"Peshlakai! Been a long time my brother." Paleo walked over and grabbed Peshlakai's outstretched hand with both his hands. He felt a deep connection with the old Navajo.

"Just like old times Paleo, when you and Mr. T worked the flea markets in Gallup and Farmington during your college

123

years."

Peshlakai looked at Paleo, who felt more like blood kin than simply a friend he hadn't seen in a long time. He had an affection for Paleo and Mr. T that was stronger than most of his family.

"Clint, this is one of the best silversmiths in the southwest, Peshlakai. Friend of mine from my college days. He can tell us what we got in these two boxes of turquoise, and their value. He's been cutting and shaping this stuff for sixty years."

Clint reached out his hand. "Nice to meet you Mr. Peshlakai."

"And," Paleo continued, "this is my director of operations in Fort Worth, Leroy, and Mr. T's friend Salvador who's traveling through on his way west."

Peshlakai shook hands with Leroy. He felt the man's great physical strength and sensed a strong spirit.

Then he reached out to shake Salvador's hand, and spotted the coin silver bracelet he was wearing. *So, this was the kid Mr. T had told him about last night, the angry young man who fights. 'Hashkey Naabah'. Leaving home in the cloak of darkness.*

"Traveling west?", Peshlakai said as he smiled at Sal. "Lots of space to feel the wind in your hair and the sun on your face."

Salvador shook the hand of the old Navajo, whose face appeared to be etched by the forces of nature, and whose eyes reflected the passing of time. *Yes, he was traveling west. Running from the law. Running from his past.*

CHAPTER 37

Marcy stared at the mirror while she applied the makeup that would hide her sadness. Or at least part of it. She noticed the dark circles around her eyes and wondered if she would ever feel normal again.

Looking around her bedroom, she gazed at every picture of her son, her only son. From the time he was a baby to the time he became a senior in high school. Her eyes stopped at the picture she'd taken of Sal and Zane a few weeks ago, working on the 1962 Chevy Wagon.

What had she done wrong in raising him? Why did the judge decide to make him an example, even though he was protecting Samantha from a predator? Where was he now, and was he safe? Would she ever see him again?

The questions poured through her mind relentlessly, day after day.

"STOP!", she yelled at herself in the mirror. *Go to work. Be positive. Be strong. Stay busy.* This was her new reality, and she fought to stay focused every day.

It was Saturday morning and Marcy arrived at the Waffle

House at 5 am for her early shift. As she entered, she looked toward the back booth and spotted Troy. It only took one glance to know that Troy had new information he wanted to share with her.

After doing the required kitchen prep work, Marcy ordered Troy breakfast and brought him a cup of coffee. She sat down in the booth and looked at him, anxious for any news about Sal.

The front door to the restaurant flew open and Samantha rushed in. Wide-eyed, she walked hurriedly over to Marcy and sat down. "Any news yet?"

Marcy shook her head no. Sam threw her arms around Marcy and wept bitterly. After several minutes, her tears turned to whimpers and she lifted up her head, reaching for a napkin. She dried her eyes and grabbed Marcy's hand.

Troy remained quiet until he felt that both Samantha and Marcy were ready to listen. He decided not to tell them that the corrupt judge assigned to Salvador, along with a few heavy weights in the police department, were scheming to move Sal swiftly through the court system and into jail. Instead, he'd deliver a message of hope, give them something they could hang on to.

"Mornin' Marcy, mornin' Sam. Just wanted to come by for a few minutes and let y'all know that I've got a couple of leads as to where Sal might be, so I'll be gone for a few days. When I get back, I'll give you an update. Until then, Salvador needs you to be strong. Keep working, keep hoping."

Troy's breakfast arrived at the table. Marcy reached out with her right hand, squeezed Troy's arm, then went back to work.

Samantha followed Marcy and gave her a long hug by the register. Marcy watched as Sam exited the restaurant and got into her mom's car.

Marcy had cried all the tears she had in her body, and now she'd go through the motions of work. And the motions of life at home. There was nothing to do now but wait. And hope. And stay busy.

CHAPTER 38

Clint, Paleo, Leroy and Salvador gathered around the table, watching the Native American silversmith look through the boxes of turquoise.

Peshlakai picked up each piece and turned it over in his hands. Next, he laid the rough specimens on the table in separate piles, until the complete collection lay on display in front of them.

"They're from an old collection," Peshlakai stated. "Looks to be from the classic turquoise mines of the southwest. Cerrillos, Morenci, Sleeping Beauty, #8, Kingman, Lone Mountain, Bisbee, and a few others."

"I've placed them in four piles, according to value. This pile, $1 a gram. This one, $2 a gram, and this one, $5 a gram. Now, this large pile might be from Lone Mountain and Bisbee. Can be a little pricey. $10 to $25 a gram, or more."

Paleo had worked with Peshlakai in the past. He was familiar with his extensive knowledge of turquoise and his reputation of impeccable honesty in business. "Peshlakai, pick out the specimens you want and we'll cut you a deal. Clint's in 'em light so we can work with you on the price."

Peshlakai eased over to the $2 pile and selected several pieces. "These are the only ones I need for my inventory. You should charge me about $2 a gram."

Paleo reached into his fishing vest for the small scale he kept with him and placed the specimens on the scale.

"Looks like about 150 grams, multiplied times two equals $300. But for you Peshlakai, $50. And don't argue. We got plenty to sell and lots of chili in the pot."

Clint stepped up to the table. "Excuse me, Peshlakai. Here's an additional thank you for pricing the two boxes." Clint reached over to the Bisbee-Lone Mountain stack and handed Peshlakai five medium-sized specimens.

"I got lucky on this deal, and I don't like to be greedy. Besides, Paleo said you are family. 'Preciate the business." Clint and Peshlakai shook hands.

"Thank you." Peshlakai nodded to Clint then turned toward Paleo.

"Paleo, next time you come through the reservation, please stop by. Mr. T will give you my address. There's something hidden behind my hogan that you will be interested in."

They shook hands and Peshlakai walked away, disappearing into the crowd of dealers.

CHAPTER 39

It was 8:00 am and the trading was just starting to heat up when Paleo walked over to Salvador with a grin on his face.

"Salvador, good news on the antique rifle you caught fishing in the Trinity. Found out it's an 1873 Winchester with special features. And, there's an identifiable signature from a military officer in the U.S. Army. Got two cash offers on the table, north of $1,000."

Leroy let out a long whistle. "Salvador, you might have the tradin' magic."

Sal grinned and wondered how a piece of old rusted metal in the river could be worth so much money. He didn't know if Paleo was teasing him, or if he was serious.

"Leroy, looks like everything's set up for the sale today. Go ahead and take Sal around the market, show him the ropes. Try to be back around noon so we can head over to the Henderson Flea and set up for Sunday."

Leroy and Sal headed out into the sea of traders. The scent of fresh roasting peppers filled the air.

Sal looked at Leroy. "Paleo said when we got to Fort

Worth you might tell me the secret to finding dinosaur bones."

Leroy nodded. "Yeah, he mentioned that to me yesterday. I was gonna tell you last night, but we fell asleep. But the secret's probably not what you think it is."

Sal had a quizzical but eager look on his face.

"The secret is…you gotta look for them."

Salvador's face changed from anticipation to disappointment.

Leroy laughed. "Sorry Sal, but people ask us that all the time, and my answer is always the same, whether its dinosaur bones or antiques. You just gotta get out there and see what you can find. Now…let's go work the market."

They walked the entire length and depth of Traders Village, stopping at every tent or table that caught Leroy's eye.

They traded for Nocona cowboy boots and a box of vinyl records from the '60's. They bought a rusted Mobil gasoline sign, five pairs of ripped denim overalls, and three standup microphones from the '50's.

They also picked up a beat-up acoustic guitar, a very old Hopi pot with a signature on the bottom and a small 1940's brown tweed overnight case filled with an assortment of silver and costume jewelry.

"Not bad pickin' today Sal. Got a good mix of smalls and bigs. That guitar you found under them boxes is a vintage Gibson from the '40s. Money in the bank!"

"How'd you get so much knowledge about all this stuff Leroy?"

"First, from my mom Thelma, smartest woman I know. We hit the sales every weekend since I was a kid. Also learned a lot from Paleo and Chen. They taught me to watch traders closely and listen. I also read a lot."

Leroy continued. "I don't spend time worrying about

makin' mistakes. I've made plenty. Those have been my best teachers. The pain from makin' bad trades tell me that I'm only as good as my next trade. Keeps me humble. Cautious. Patient."

A man in a wheelchair pulled in front of Leroy and stopped. He was wearing jean shorts, flip-flops, and a long-sleeve Nike sports hoodie that read: 'Just Do It'. His penetrating blue eyes were complemented by neatly trimmed hair, wire rim glasses, and a blackish grey goatee.

Attached to the back of the wheelchair was a 1' x 1' foot metal license plate stating the name of the trader: "*WHEELS MCCOY*".

Wheels looked at Leroy. "Paleo said you found something for me at the Henderson Market last month Leroy. Got it with you?"

Leroy smiled and reached into his backpack, pulled out a small blue velvet whiskey bag and handed it to the man in the wheelchair. "Here you go Mr. McCoy. See what you think."

Wheels took the sack and pulled out a pair of rusted metal spurs. Next, he got a magnifying glass out of his front pocket and examined every inch of each spur. A small grin spread across his face.

"Unbelievable. Just like Paleo described. J.O. BASS spurs from Tulia, Texas. Made in the early 1900's in his blacksmith shop in Quitaque. You got a number in mind?"

"Well, Mr. McCoy, you'll have to talk with Paleo. He's already traded me out of them spurs. Offered me two tickets to the Cowboys-Eagles home game this year, front row seats on the fifty-yard line. I've never been to a Cowboys game, so I jumped on that deal faster than a chicken on a June bug."

McCoy grinned. "Much appreciated Leroy. Tell Paleo to keep his tradin' shorts on. He knows these old spurs are my weakness. See you guys next week. Go Cowboys."

Wheels quickly spun his wheelchair around and rode away. Leroy looked over at Sal.

"Sal, you just got to see the best trader in the metroplex, Wheels McCoy. Ex-green beret, ex-CEO of a large company in California, ex-congressman. A competition surfer in his younger days. And, one of the biggest legends in the history of Traders Village."

"How long has he been in a wheelchair?" asked Sal.

"Thirty-five years. Injured in combat on a special mission, but he won't talk about it. I heard about it from his son who came by a few years ago. He said that *Wheels* decided he was not going to let his injury define him. No excuses. He don't want pity from nobody."

Leroy pulled out a pocket watch. "Whoa! It's 12:15pm. Time to roll. Paleo's probably waiting on us. Gotta set up for the Henderson market tomorrow."

CHAPTER 40

By early afternoon Paleo, Leroy, and Sal were squeezed into the cab of the El Camino. The bed of the vehicle was loaded with fresh merchandise for the Henderson Market.

Paleo took the Montgomery Street exit off I-30 west and drove to his favorite lunch spot, Whataburger. "Green-Chili Double! Is there a better burger in Texas Leroy?"

"If there is I ain't had it yet."

Standing in line, Leroy looked over at Sal. "Ever had a Green-Chili Double?"

"Never. First time I've eaten here since I was a young boy. I wouldn't mind trying one."

Paleo stepped up to the register. "Three Green-Chili Doubles, three fries, three cokes."

Their order arrived at the table quickly. Silence descended while they worked their way through the meal.

Paleo pushed his chair back and looked over at Sal.

"Salvador, it's been nice having you around. Feels like you're part of our family. I know you've got to leave in a few days. Mr. T's told me all about your situation. But if you come back through and want to work with us, just let me know. Me and Leroy's already talked about it. Chen's on board too."

Sal smiled at the two traders. "Thanks Paleo, Leroy. But I didn't know people made a career out of working at flea markets and antique shows. I been wondering the past few days how you and Chen and Leroy pay your debts."

Paleo and Leroy looked at each other.

"What debt? Everything we have is paid for. There's a small weekend fee for the space at Henderson, and I pay my yearly income taxes in February. That's it. Clint pays for two storage facilities at Traders Village, and he lets us store some of our merchandise there. We sleep in a tent."

Sal looked dumbfounded.

"Look Sal, I left college about the same time that Bill Gates dropped out of Harvard and moved to Albuquerque. Hell, Steve Jobs didn't even go to college."

Paleo continued. "Like those two tech guys, I decided I was gonna do work that fascinated me. Dinosaurs. Driftin'. Flea Markets. Antiques. Be my own boss."

"I learned quick that my chances of being successful were good if I didn't owe anybody money. So, I paid cash for everything, or traded for it. If I couldn't pay or trade for it, I wouldn't get it."

Paleo took a drink of his coke. "I've operated like that for thirty-five years, working six to seven days a week. Ate lots of rice and beans. Chen's been doing it for ten years and Leroy for five."

Thinking about the decades of hard work, Paleo built up steam for his story. "Last time I was at the bank, I had $200,000 in savings and $50,000 in checking. I own a trailer fully furnished on five acres in Quartzsite, a '59 Chevy El Camino, a '66 mustang, and a sixteen-foot Bambi Airstream

RV."

"My business inventory includes more than 10,000 antiques, collectables, and dinosaur specimens. And no debt."

Paleo became animated as he spoke. The passion in his voice was palpable.

"La Reunion trades with ALL the major antique stores and dealers in the Dallas-Fort Worth Metroplex, but we do have our favorites. In Dallas it's LULA B'S and Curiosities. In Fort Worth we like the Cattle Barn Flea and Montgomery Street Antiques."

Sal was astonished, and curious. He looked over at Leroy.

"So, Leroy, you've been working the markets for about five years?"

Leroy nodded, "When I got injured the army gave me a little money. I took out a small amount of cash and put the rest in savings. Spent three months in the hospital, recuperating from my injury. Did a lot of reading. Thinking. Praying. God led me to live on the river and work with the homeless. I needed to heal my mind from the war."

Leroy wiped his mouth with his napkin. "I worked with the homeless every day for three months on the river. My mind began to heal, so I started thinking about getting a job. And that's when I met Paleo and Chen. They showed me how to work the business."

"I'm 24 years old now. I've got $30,000 in savings, $7,000 in checking, and a business inventory of 5,000 antiques and collectables. And no debt. I buy and sell, I trade, I save. Work six to seven days a week, same as Paleo and Chen."

Sal looked out the window, trying to make sense of these homeless guys who'd dropped out of society and forged a career out of nothing. Buying and selling and trading. Living on the margins. Doing what they love.

CHAPTER 41

Henderson Bazaar was packed when they drove up. Paleo eased the El Camino toward the north side of the market and pulled his vehicle up to the edge of the awning. Leroy got out and picked up the *RESERVED* sign from the parking spot, which was strategically located just across from where their '76 cargo van sat.

"Y'all seem to be runnin' a little late today Leroy. Paleo might be getting too old for this business. Goin' senile." It was a dealer close by, evidently one that knew Paleo and Leroy.

"Socrates, you old shriveled up, four-eyed, book-tradin' codger." Paleo walked over and shook the man's hand affectionately.

At age 84, Socrates stood with the help of a cane. Through damaged glasses held together by black electrical tape he examined the new inventory in the back of Paleo's vehicle.

"I got about two dollars I'll give you for all of it. Might come up to three if you throw in the old beat up Gibson."

Paleo laughed. "Leroy, we gotta get this stuff in the step-van before any other tight wad comes around blowin' hot air."

Leroy picked up several boxes and carried them to the van. Sal did the same. Within fifteen minutes they had unloaded the entire contents from the El Camino.

Sal watched as Paleo walked down the asphalt road close to the fence and disappear around the corner.

Leroy approached Socrates table and began slowly rummaging through the books, and Sal decided to join him. The first book he came to was called *Reily's Luck*, written by Louis L'Amour. He picked it up and read several pages. It was a story about a little boy and a gambler in the American West.

"Louis L'Amour, best western writer in history." Socrates adjusted his glasses. "And *Reily's Luck* is one of his best. Careful about reading L'Amour. Can be addictive."

Leroy picked up the three books from his pile and handed them to Socrates. "Believe I'll take these three for me and this one for Sal. Still $1 per book Socrates?"

"Not today Leroy. You've already bought over thirty books this month. These four are on the house. How many books do you have now in your '76 Step Side library?"

"About 800. Read every one cover to cover. Some twice."

Salvador followed Leroy toward the back of the market where he stopped by an open space next to a large dumpster.

"This is our spot Sal. We need to go over to the tent and get your sleeping bag ready for the night. Then we'll come back and do a little pickin' before Rick rolls up."

Leroy led Sal through a gap in the fence next to the dumpster and out across a grassy area. Soon they were walking on the railroad tracks that led to the bridge and across the river.

Halfway across the bridge they heard a loud splash in the water below. A young college-aged couple became frantic as their dog had jumped off their canoe and into the river. They were coaxing him back to the boat.

Leroy and Sal looked over the rails of the bridge and saw the couple yelling loudly for their dog, who was now swimming under the bridge about 15 feet from the canoe.

Suddenly the dog disappeared, followed by an agitated swirl of water and the long black tail of an alligator.

The girl screamed at the top of her voice. "Alligator! Alligator!"

Without hesitation, Leroy stepped to the edge of the bridge and plunged twenty feet into the river below.

CHAPTER 42

Leroy hit the water feet first, his weight carrying him to the bottom of the river. With legs bent to cushion the landing, Leroy pushed off the bottom and collided directly into the mid-section of the gator.

Instinctually, he grabbed the body of the creature with his powerful arms and rolled onto it's back, trying to keep distance from its deadly jaws.

Releasing his left arm, he moved his hand toward its mouth and felt the body of the small dog as it struggled to release itself from the steel grip of the alligator's teeth. He squeezed the gators midsection and pulled at its mouth.

The air in Leroy's lungs was about depleted and panic came over him. Finally, he felt the jaws of the gator release its victim and its powerful body dive down to the bottom.

At that moment Leroy pushed himself away from the alligator and powered upward. Breaking the surface, he gasped for air.

Aware of the danger beneath him, Leroy swam as fast as he could to the north shore of the Trinity River. When he reached the shore, he crawled out onto the bank and collapsed.

Sal had hurried off the bridge as soon as Leroy jumped into the river and was standing on the north bank. He grabbed Leroy and pulled him into a patch of grass. Leroy was heaving powerfully to get air into his lungs.

Looking out onto the river, Sal noticed the small dog floating with the current, blood covering its thick coat of fur. The young couple quickly positioned their boat next to the dog and were lifting its limp and mangled body out of the water. Its chest was barely moving.

The young girl sobbed, kissing the dogs' head. Her boyfriend guided the boat to shore where they laid the puppy on a dry blanket and dressed the wounds. Roscoe was hanging on to life by a thread.

Then, in his body's last attempt at life, Roscoe's breathing increased, and his eyes opened. He coughed up water several times. And gathering what strength he had left in his body, he attempted to stand. His feeble, water-drenched legs wobbled around for a few minutes before plopping down on the bank.

But the force of life was back in him now, and Roscoe breathed in deeply. It appeared he would make it.

The girl walked over to Leroy and propelled herself into his arms. "Thanks for saving our dog! You have no idea how grateful I am that you risked your life today. We will never forget you!"

CHAPTER 43

It was mid-afternoon when the men returned to the Henderson Market, and the crowd was beginning to thin out.

Paleo looked out onto the parking lot. "Rick's pulling up. Let's get there before the line gets big." They picked up their tacos and sat on the tailgate of the El Camino, exhausted from the events of the day.

Their solitude was interrupted by Socrates. "Paleo, a guy came by asking about Salvador. Had a serious look on his face. Sounded urgent."

Sal tensed up and threw a question at Socrates. "How was he dressed?"

"Wore a fishing hat and a t-shirt with the American Flag. Talked with a deep East Texas accent. He headed over to the concrete bridge by Henderson Street." Socrates pointed in that direction.

TROY WAS HERE. "Back in a few minutes Paleo."

Sal jumped off the tailgate of the vehicle and walked to the river where Troy was sitting on the bank, rod and reel in hand. Casting out like a man with not a care in the world. Sal eased down in the grass beside him.

Troy looked over. *"How you doin' Sal?"*

"Trying to make it the best I can. How'd you find me?"

"It wasn't too hard. Got lots of contacts on the street. Anyway, I talked with your mom and Samantha yesterday, told 'em I was 'gonna checkup on you. They're worried sick."

Sal asked a question that weighed heavy on his mind. "That man from Florida die?"

"Still in critical condition, but that's not the reason I came by. I wanted to let you know that a few head honchos at the police station, along with the judge they assigned to your case, found out you skipped town. By the end of the day tomorrow, they'll have some undercover cops lookin' for you. You won't be safe here."

Sal sat nervously, looking out at the river.

Troy reeled in his line and turned toward Sal. "Sal, if I was you, I'd 'ride the dog'."

"'Ride the dog'?"

"Take the first bus out of Fort Worth in the morning. Go where there's lots of open country. West to El Paso or north to Amarillo."

"Never been to either place."

Troy shrugged. "If it was ME...I'd probably head north on 287. Fewer police, and you can hit the wide-open spaces quickly."

Troy scanned the area, fidgeting, unsure if the police were tailing him in order to find Sal. "Remember Sal, this may all blow over in a year or so, and it could be safe to come back to Dallas. Just keep a low profile...and be careful." Troy shook Sal's hand and walked back to his truck.

Ride the Dog. Head north on 287. They're coming after you. Pieces of Troy's conversation echoed in Sal's mind.

Sal rushed back to where Leroy and Paleo were eating.

"Paleo...Leroy...I've got to leave town first thing in the morning...first bus out of Fort Worth. I'm going back to the tent for the rest of the night. I'll organize my stuff and stay 'til mornin'. Thanks for all your help."

Paleo and Leroy nodded, but asked no questions. There was no reaction, no emotion. Just an acknowledgement of what was said. How many times had they seen guys on the run disappear, leaving at a moment's notice?

It was the way of life along the river.

CHAPTER 44

Sal headed down the banks of the river at a brisk pace. As he crossed the bridge his eyes scanned the parking lot and Henderson street for any sign of the police. Seeing none, he entered the tent.

As dusk descended, Salvador stretched out and thought about his situation. His mind raced wildly. He was unable to sleep. Finally he gave up on rest, opened his backpack and pulled out the box his mom had given him before he left home.

He had time tonight. Time to organize his meager belongings. Time to create an exit strategy. And time to read about his father and a past that had haunted him since childhood.

Salvador opened the box and spread out the secrets to his past that had been hidden for years, worn from handling by his mom. There were old photographs, letters, keepsakes, and a few small leather bags that may help him discover who his father was and where he came from.

First, he started with the pictures. There was his mom as a young woman, stunningly attractive. Beside her was a medium built young man. Ruggedly handsome with long-hair, and a serious look in his eyes. They were nestled closely together on a beach. Smiling. Happy. In love.

Next, he picked up a stack of letters, unbound them, and opened the one with the oldest date. It was a letter from his father to his mom:

'Marcy, I have no words to describe the feelings I have for you. From the moment I first saw you in Isla Mujeres…sitting at a small table on the narrow-cobbled streets, eating pizza…I stopped dead in my tracks, eyes fixed on beauty I'd only read about in books…as if I was gazing at the Mayan goddess Ishmal incarnate….

Salvador read every word of every letter. Some he read twice. He touched every keepsake and memento. He cried, he laughed, he cursed.

In the process of going through the box, Salvador felt a deep connection to his father, who'd come from a long line of travelers and traders and archaeologist in the Middle East.

And he developed a new appreciation for his mother. She'd found herself in a difficult situation and tried to make the best of it.

His thoughts quickly moved back to his own dilemma. On the run, uncertain of which path to take, trying to find direction for his life. He wondered if his father's career path as an archeologist might someday become his path. He liked the idea of travel and the study of ancient history.

But his most pressing problem was deciding which direction to take out of Fort Worth. Which path would help him disappear, and keep him from being arrested? West toward El Paso, or north on 287 toward Amarillo?

After deliberating for almost an hour, he made his decision. He'd take the bus north to Amarillo. From there, he might strike out west to New Mexico and explore the land of turquoise that Paleo had talked about.

Salvador lay there that night on the banks of the river, feeling the emptiness of being alone, mixed with an anticipation of what his new life would entail.

CHAPTER 45

"Salvador…Salvador…Salvador, wake up!"

Salvador slowly raised his head, not fully conscious. He heard a voice calling his name. Felt a strong hand shaking his shoulder. "Salvador, time to wake up. Need to pack all your stuff."

He rubbed the sleep from his eyes and noticed that Leroy had turned on the small tent lamp. He looked around and saw the contents of the box strewn about haphazardly. He must have dozed off late last night.

Sal packed the contents of the box and placed it in his backpack before exiting the tent. It was still dark outside, a hint of light rising in the east.

"Sal, there's several news vans that just showed up on the parking lot of the Henderson Market. Somehow, they got wind of the alligator incident yesterday. They're wanting to interview both of us and take pictures for their newspapers."

"And, there's rumors that someone took pictures of us walking on the bridge across the river, just before I jumped in to save Roscoe."

Leroy reached into his pocket and pulled out a key. "Here's a key to a bicycle I keep locked and hidden under the old concrete Henderson bridge. The bike will get you to the bus station quickly."

"To find the bike, take the path just behind the tent that leads to the cemetery. Continue west into the thick vegetation of a small forested area. You'll run directly into it, snuggled up to a metal post under the bridge. Unlock the bike and follow a narrow concrete ledge that leads to Henderson Avenue."

Leroy looked around cautiously to see if anyone was approaching.

"Once on Henderson, head north to the first light, University. Left on University to 7th Avenue, then toward downtown. You'll cross the railroad track and a small bridge. Go all the way through the city until you dead end at the bus station."

Salvador went over the directions in his mind. Path behind tent to the bridge. Henderson. University. 7th street to the downtown bus station.

"One last thing. Paleo left this envelop with your money from the sale of that old rifle you pulled out of the river."

Half asleep, Sal shoved the envelop into his backpack.

Leroy reached out his powerful hand and placed it on Sal's shoulder. "Brother Salvador, time to hit the trail. Like my father use to say, *'You rollin' with G' now."*

PART FOUR

RIDE THE DOG

CHAPTER 46

Brendon Holloway dropped the newspaper on the counter and scanned the room for the young reporter he had scheduled a meeting with.

"Morning Mr. Holloway. Grande dark with room and a blueberry muffin?"

Brendon nodded and smiled at the barista. "And the local paper."

He picked up his coffee and headed over to his window chair that looked out toward 7th Avenue in downtown Fort Worth. Took a big bite of the warm blueberry muffin and picked up the paper.

He examined the headlines: "HOMELESS MILITARY HERO RISKS LIFE TO SAVE DOG IN THE TRINITY RIVER." Soon he was rereading the story, looking for more details.

The pictures of the homeless man splashed across the front page of the local paper seemed familiar. Like someone he'd seen before. Or interviewed. Maybe a former football star he'd covered on one of his many Friday night trips around

Texas.

He knew this guy. He was sure of it. Long ago he'd learn to trust his instincts.

The door opened and in walked the writer of the article. An earthy lookin' guy. About 5'-10". Skinny with unruly hair and a relaxed set of eyes. Very young.

"Mornin' Mr. Holloway. Be right there." He picked up his coffee and made his way to the chair next to Brendon.

"Great article Scott. The kind of story that can catapult a career in journalism."

The young reporter beamed at the compliment from one of Texas's most celebrated sports writers.

"Thanks. But I'll have to say that I'm surprised you wanted to meet me. I'm just a greenhorn freelance writer drifting around the state, snapping pictures on a whim. Covering things that interest me. Not even sure I want a career in journalism."

Brendon smiled, remembering his own unimpressive start as a sportswriter.

"Don't really matter. You nailed this story. I drove down Henderson this morning on my way here. Saw lots of news vans from around the state parked by the river, trying to get more information about this homeless vet."

Brendon got up and asked for another shot of gusto. He was beginning to get excited. Even after fifty years, he still loved the thrill of excavating unknown pieces of a fascinating story.

"You told me on the phone that you had several more pictures related to this story. More pictures of the homeless vet, and another guy he was walking with before he jumped into the river."

Scott put the coffee down and opened his cheap, well-used

153

laptop. He hit a few keys. Pictures slowly appeared on the screen.

"Yea. Took several pictures of the scene. Didn't know at the time I'd write an article and submit it to the local paper. *Matter of fact I'm heading back down to Henderson street later today and see if I can find out who that other drifter was. Like to get his story.*"

The young journalist picked up the laptop and handed it to Brendon.

"Here you go. Just scroll up and down. There're about 20 pictures. Some of the young couple and the dog. Some of the vet. Even took a few pictures of the other guy walking with the vet."

Brendon eagerly took the laptop and closely examined the pictures. There were about seven photos of the homeless military veteran. He examined each picture closely and began to make some connections. He did know this guy, he was sure of it.

He sat the laptop down, grabbed his pen and scribbled some notes on a coffee-stained Starbucks napkin.

"Your article said his name is Leroy. That right?"

Scott nodded. "Yea. That's what an old man at the flea market told me. Said Leroy's a dealer at the market. Highly respected. Hard worker that will give you the shirt off his back, but not someone to mess with."

Brendon examined the picture on the front of the newspaper and tried to remember the name of this former Texas high school football player. He picked up his coffee and looked out the window, watching a young guy on a bicycle riding toward downtown. And that's when it came to him.

Leroy was a star tailback from the Texas panhandle. Exploded on the sports scene out of nowhere, playing football only during his senior year of high school. Ran a 4.38 forty-yard dash. Offered a full scholarship to play for a Division One team in Texas, which he turned down in order to join the military.

But Leroy wasn't the name.

"Scott, I'll be in touch. Here's a small thank you for showing me these pictures." Brendon dropped a hundred-dollar bill on the table and walked out of the 7th street Starbucks in downtown Ft. Worth.

CHAPTER 47

Sal headed down the dirt path behind the tent. On past the cemetery and into a small but dense cluster of trees and vegetation. In the dim light of the early morning he tripped over a drunk sprawled out on the ground. The man mumbled incoherently but barely moved.

Soon he came upon the bike. He quickly unlocked it, pushed it up the concrete embankment, and rode down Henderson to University. Left on University to 7th Avenue, which took him across the bridge and into the heart of the city.

Just before the 7th street bridge, he saw the lights of a local Starbucks, and a few customers sitting by the window. He was cold and sleepy and hungry.

Should he stop?

His desire was strong, but he pressed on across the railroad tracks and the Trinity River Bridge. Past massive skyscrapers that stood like giants in a forest. All the way through blocks and blocks of concrete 'til he reached a dead end.

Where was the bus station?

He looked left but saw no signs of movement or human

activity, so he decided to take Jones street south. Success. He got off his bike, leaned it against the building, and walked inside the station.

Several people were scattered about in the lobby. Some were reading, some sleeping. Others looked like drifters. But there was a small group of travelers that made him feel uneasy. They were fidgeting and staring at him in a challenging way.

Keep your head on a swivel. Keep moving. Avoid dangerous situations. Ahmad's words rang out in his mind.

He maneuvered around the predators and drifters, following the signs to the ticket counter.

"One ticket to Amarillo."

The bus clerk appeared disinterested. "I need your driver's license and one hundred and five dollars."

Anxiety streak through his body. Would the ticket clerk be able to tell if his license was fake?

He pulled out his newly acquired driver's license and placed it on the counter, along with the money. The clerk looked closely at his ID for several seconds before handing it back.

"Thank you, Mr. Landry. Bus leaves in fifty-five minutes."

Looking around the lobby, he picked out a place away from the others and moved quickly to a chair. He noticed a man seated across the room, eyeballing him suspiciously while he made his way to sit down.

He checked his backpack, made sure everything was there. Looked around the room for the exits in case he had to move quickly, then up at the clock. *Fifty minutes to departure.*

Unzipping his backpack, he pulled out one of the books Mr. T had given him just before he left Dallas. *Education of a Wandering Man*, by Louis L'Amour.

Hmmm…same author as the book that Leroy had bought him at the flea market. Eagerly he began to read chapter one, stopping on page four. He went back and reread one of the paragraphs, wanting to make sure he'd read it correctly.

L 'Amour quit school in the tenth grade...school was getting in the way of his education.

The man across the room continued to stare.

CHAPTER 48

Sal had gotten lucky, as he had a window seat with no passenger sitting beside him.

Once everyone boarded, the bus eased out of the parking lot and down the streets of Fort Worth. Away from the city and onto highway 287 north towards Decatur.

The buildings and the traffic thinned out, and soon they were traveling past rolling hills and grasslands. Tall skyscrapers and concrete had been replaced by cattle and windmills. Sal felt his body slowing down.

The tranquility of the moment was briefly interrupted by movement and voices coming from two suspicious looking characters across the aisle to his right.

Both stared at him. Only one spoke.

"Hey man. Got a cigarette?"

"No, I don't smoke."

"Got a few extra bucks I can borrow?"

Sal felt irritated. "I'm broke. Ain't got nothin'."

"Damn! You sure?"

Both drifters stared at Sal's backpack he'd put in the seat

beside him. They seemed agitated as they looked up and down the aisle of the bus.

"Yeah, I'm sure."

The intercom crackled when the bus driver spoke:

"First stop in sixty minutes. Wichita Falls."

Salvador reached for his backpack and pulled out the novel Leroy bought him at the Henderson market, *Reilly's Luck*. He then placed his backpack away from the aisle, next to the window, and began to read.

Sal quickly found himself engrossed in the story of a young homeless boy and a gambler drifting through the American West during the 1800's. This was the first western he'd ever read.

Socrates told him to be careful. Reading Louis L'Amour could be addictive.

After reading several chapters he decided to put the book away. In the process of unzipping his backpack an envelope fell out and landed on the floor next to the aisle. *Several twenty-dollar bills were exposed.* It was the envelope from Paleo that Leroy had given him.

The two travelers across the aisle stared at the exposed money, then looked up at Sal. They whispered to each other, then stared back at the money.

I've got to be more careful, he told himself.

He quickly picked up the envelope and began to shove the twenty's back when he noticed a letter inside.

He pulled out the letter and placed the envelope into his pocket. It was a letter from Paleo.

'Sal. Here's $900 from that old rifle you pulled out of the river. I sold it to a collector from Tennessee for $1200. I kept 25% of the sale, my standard fee for brokering a deal.'

He looked out the window, barely able to comprehend

how an old rusted piece of junk could be worth that much money. He continued to read the letter.

'One thing we forgot to do while you were here was give you a ROAD NAME. Comes in handy when you're traveling under the radar. We all have one: Paleo, Chen, Leroy, Socrates. If you're not sure how to pick a name, just think about a character in a book, movie or cartoon. One word only. And change the spelling.'

A cartoon. *YOGI BEAR.* Watched it with his uncle when he was a kid. *YOGI.* Get a unique spelling. *Y-O-G-E-E.* Sal pronounced the word quietly to himself as he scribbled it out on the letter.

YOGEE. That's it! He liked the sound of the name, how it rolled easily off his tongue.

Next thing he heard was the voice of the bus driver:

"*Wichita Falls, Texas. Everybody off. We'll re-board in twenty minutes.*"

CHAPTER 49

Salvador stepped off the bus and made his way toward the north end of the terminal. He sat down on the grass and leaned against a two-foot limestone bench close to a security officer.

As he had anticipated, the two drifters followed, but stopped when they saw the guard. Turning quickly, they headed in the opposite direction toward Pat's Drive-In.

Gentle south winds and a warm spring sun eased the tension in his body. The soft grass added to the feeling of comfort, and he pulled out the Louis L'Amour novel he was reading on the bus.

The story moved quickly, and soon he was lost in another world. Gunfighters and gamblers. Drifters on horseback riding across the great landscapes of the west.

Somewhere along the way he began to get drowsy. Having had almost no sleep in the tent from the night before, he slid down further in the thick carpet-like grass, stretched out his legs, and placed his backpack under his head.

His eyes were heavy. Soon he was fast asleep.

HONK! HONK! He jumped up, heart racing. A car on Scott Avenue in front of the bus station was laying on the horn.

He looked around and noticed all the passengers on the bus were gone. The place was empty. He began to panic!

Backpack? Where was his backpack? Sal found it right where he'd put it, leaning against the rock bench. He bent down and checked the contents.

Everything was there. He harnessed the pack on his shoulders and felt for the money in his pocket, and the money belt around his waist. Lucky this time. He cursed loudly at himself!

"You idiot! You better start paying attention to what's going on or they'll be pulling your dead ass out of a dumpster."

Moving with urgency, Salvador made his way toward the station. Before entering the building, he looked up at the clock tower. 11:45am. He'd slept for almost an hour.

Walking into the station he saw a uniformed employee reading a newspaper, drinking coffee.

"Ma'am, when's the next bus come through to Amarillo?"

The employee looked up. "Not till tomorrow morning."

He cursed at himself again under his breath. Tomorrow? What was he going to do till tomorrow? And where was he going to sleep tonight?

Though his mind was fresh from the sleep he'd just had, he was very hungry. He hadn't eaten since yesterday afternoon.

"Can you tell me where there's a place to eat close by?"

She put down the paper. "Pat's Drive-In is just across the street. Good hamburgers."

A hamburger sounded good, but then he remembered that the two drifters on the bus had gone in that direction. "Is there another place that's close by where I can get a burger?"

163

"Well, if you're not in a big hurry you can walk down Scott Avenue north to Kenley. It's about eight blocks. Turn right on Kenley and you'll run right into a What-A-Burger. It's just off 287 north. Stay's open 24-7."

"Thanks."

Out of the station and down Scott Avenue. Lots of traffic and drifters along this corridor. He kept a fast pace, his eyes scanning for any sign of trouble.

He crossed a river and traveled under a freeway bridge. Once past the bridge he began to look for Kenley. He found it and turned right. Within a few blocks he arrived.

CHAPTER 50

"Can I help you sir?"

Sal was looking at the menu board above the employee's head. "I'd like a green-chili double, fries and a coke."

"That'll be $7.49." She took the money and gave Sal a number.

He found an open table in the back corner with a view of highway 287. Pulling off his backpack, he dug out the book he'd been reading. Socrates was right. L'Amour was addictive.

Within a few minutes his order arrived. He was starving and tore into the meal. The green-chili double disappeared. He leaned back, relaxed and looked around the restaurant. The place was packed. Not a single table open.

Looking out the window, he began to think about his dilemma. Where would he sleep tonight? Under a bridge? On the banks of the river he crossed on Scott Avenue? An empty parking lot?

Suddenly another problem occurred to him. Where was he going to stay when he arrived in Amarillo? And what was he going to do?

For now, he'd relax and read his novel. Then walk the

streets of Wichita Falls and find a place to sleep for the night.

"SALVADOR GONZALEZ!" *A deep, authoritative voice called his name.*

CHAPTER 51

Sal's body froze and his breathing became shallow. His hand clamped down on the book.

How did the police find him so quickly?

He released the book and placed his hands in full site on the table. He would not resist his arrest. He'd accept his fate.

Without looking up, he noticed the form of a man ease into the bench opposite his. Slowly, he lifted his eyes. The first thing he noticed was the arm of a man wearing an old silver bracelet, similar in style to the one he was wearing.

He quickly lifted his head and stared at the person across from him. *Peshlakai! Turquoise trader he'd met at the flea market.*

"You look like you've just seen a ghost. Mind if I join you for lunch?" Without waiting for an answer, Peshlakai sat down and plowed into his meal.

Sal breathed in deeply, then let out a long sigh of relief. "I thought the police had found me and were going to arrest me. Take me back to Dallas. Put me on trial for murder. Then lock me up for twenty-five years."

Peshlakai looked up from eating and nodded his head. He

reached across the table and picked up the salt and pepper, dispensing a generous portion on his half-eaten hamburger.

"Green chili double. Might be the best burger in Texas." Peshlakai smiled at Sal and continued to eat.

Sal stared at Peshlakai. He'd not known any old Native American Indians. Only read about them in books. Seen them in western movies.

But now he was seated beside one. Tanned face etched by the sun and the wind. Long greyish hair pulled back in a ponytail. Eyes that measured the passage of time. A small vintage bolo with greenish-blue turquoise lay gently on his black t-shirt. And the old bracelet.

Peshlakai stopped eating for a minute and looked at the young man across the table. *The angry warrior. Mr. T had told him that he'd severely beaten a man for attacking his girlfriend.*

"Heard you might be heading west on the bus. Surprised to see you here in Wichita Falls." Peshlakai took another big bite of his hamburger.

Salvador felt safe with Peshlakai and began to talk. He told Peshlakai about his mom, his friend Zane and his girlfriend Samantha. He told him about his fights at school and how he saw Samantha being attacked. How he lost control and almost killed a man.

Then he told Peshlakai about the police interview, his decision to leave home, Ahmad, and his time with Paleo and Chen and Leroy. And how he'd fallen asleep and missed his bus to Amarillo.

"Got a new name now. A *Road* name: *YOGEE.*"

Time seemed to pass quickly as Sal rambled on and on. He noticed Peshlakai was quiet. Observant. Listening intently. Finally Sal ran out of gas. He felt exhausted.

Peshlakai placed his trash on the tray, moved it over to the side of the table, and looked at Salvador.

"Yogee, sounds like you're in deep shit." Peshlakai chuckled as he got up from the booth.

He looked down at the young man, then shifted his eyes to the parking lot. "I'm heading to Amarillo. Plan to be there by dinner if my truck don't break down. Welcome to come if you like. Just don't expect comfort or special treatment."

CHAPTER 52

Peshlakai eased his vintage Chevy truck onto highway 287 north. *How long had it been since he last drove through Texas? About five years ago. Last time he visited his sister in Palestine.*

Sal looked around the inside of the truck. Empty coffee cups, dirty t-shirts. And a miscellaneous assortment of rocks, mud, rough turquoise specimens and dinosaur bones. Along with several 'Arizona Highway' magazines that lay ripped and heavily written upon.

A small snub-nosed pistol sat securely under the glove box, only half hidden.

Several books were scattered about, and one on the dashboard caught his eye: *Empire of the Summer Moon.* He picked it up and thumbed through it.

Peshlakai observed Sal's interest in the book and wondered if he'd learned much about the topic when he was in school. Wondered if he'd been taught anything about Native American history.

"Book came out of Mr. T's library. He loves history. Got thousands of books. He gave it to me when I stayed with him a few days ago. It's about a great Comanche chief, Quanah Parker, and how he walked two roads during his lifetime."

Sal wasn't sure what he was talking about, and it registered on his face.

Peshlakai looked at Sal, and it reminded him of his own situation as a young man. Traveling through towns and cities around the states, mostly unaware of what had happened in the past.

Those were his drifting days. Carefree. Unhurried. Following any fascination that came his way.

Without much thought or internal dialogue, Peshlakai decided to exit at the small rural town of Electra, just a few miles away. He slowed the truck and eased off 287 before heading west on highway 25. He wasn't sure if the marker would still be there.

Salvador was curious why they were heading west, since Amarillo was north. But he just figured there was a shortcut Peshlakai knew about.

They traveled down the desolate two-lane highway. Past oil rigs, cattle and broken-down pickups abandoned in the fields.

Abruptly, Peshlakai pulled the truck off the side of the road and parked by a sign. It was a historical marker that had a small story under the title: THE OLD BUFFALO ROAD.

Peshlakai eased out of the truck and leaned against the drivers' side bed. So many decades ago, and the sign was still here. And his memories of the land and the people. And a girl from Memphis, Texas.

"I used to drive out here many years ago. Park my truck and hike around the area, trying to find the Old Buffalo Road. Never did find it."

Salvador got out, walked over to the sign and read the story. He walked up and down both sides of state highway 25, looking for any remnants of the path that used to carry buffalo hides and bones to market in the late 1800's.

Fifteen minutes later he gave up and walked back to the pickup. "Probably all gone Peshlakai."

Peshlakai reached into the cab of his pickup and pulled out a well-used, faded red towel, wiping the sweat off his forehead. "Probably so. Guess we better get on down the road. Want to make Amarillo by dinnertime."

CHAPTER 53

By the time they got back on highway 287 north, Peshlakai had begun to feel the old feelings. Drifting down the open road with no agenda. No plan. No time constraints.

He rolled down the window and let the warm Texas wind ruffle his hair. An invigorating surge of energy flowed through his body.

He looked over at his young friend, who seemed to be engrossed in the book about Quanah Parker.

"287 North goes right through the old Comanche lands. They lived here for hundreds of years. Hunted the buffalo. Fought the Spanish, the Mexicans, the Texans, and finally the American settlers pushing west."

Sal looked up from the book. "What happened to Quanah Parker, the great Comanche Indian Chief?"

"There was a battle in Pala Duro Canyon. The US Military defeated the Comanche and forced them onto the reservations."

"Quanah could have kept fighting but knew he would have eventually been killed. He decided to move to the reservation and embrace the laws and customs of the white man. Over time, Quanah become one of the most successful and respected Comanches in America."

Salvador looked out the windshield, taking in the vast expanse of land as it continued to unfold. Blue skies opening into the horizons. Puffs of clouds carried by southern spring winds.

He was fascinated by the oil rigs that were spread throughout the landscape, pumping the greasy black energy from the earth. And the tall wind turbines lined up in rows into the distance.

Names of tiny Texas towns appeared along the highway. Medicine Mound. Chillicothe. Quanah. Childress.

Peshlakai eased off the gas when they approached the town of Estelline. Population, 141. Within seconds they were at the edge of the city where a huge billboard advertised a restaurant.

BIG TEXAN. FREE 72 oz STEAK.

Just past that sign they'd begun to cross a river. Peshlakai slowed the truck, looking on both sides. Intently trying to identify something.

Once across the bridge, Peshlakai pulled over and parked ten feet off the highway in a grassy area that nudged up to a group of trees.

"Goin on a little hike. Welcome to come if you like, or you can wait in the truck. Lock your door if you get out." Peshlakai grabbed a walking stick he kept behind the truck seat, shut the door and locked it.

Off he went at a quick pace, down the embankment toward the river. *He remembered what he'd found decades ago. And where.* Instinctually his feet carried him down the embankment toward his destination.

After about five minutes he stopped and looked back. Sal was struggling to keep up. He waited for him to arrive.

"Need to find you a walking stick Yogee. You might need it." He pointed to a pile of brush. "Animals get active this time of year."

Peshlakai turned and continued to trek down the Prairie Dog Town Fork of the Red River, a historic river that eons ago had carved into the earth the second largest canyon in the United States.

And a river that held secrets to the past. His past.

Sal walked over to the brush pile and selected a small tree branch, perfect for a walking stick. He pulled and something strange moved in the dirt. He looked closer.

"Peshlakai! Peshlakai!"

CHAPTER 54

Peshlakai's mind, preoccupied with memories of his youthful explorations, was interrupted by the sound of his name. He turned around. Salvador was back toward the bridge, waving wildly. Calling his name and pointing in the dirt at a pile of brush.

He stopped abruptly and made his way back to his young friend.

Kneeling by the brush pile, Sal pointed to an object covered by a mangled collection of twigs and tree branches. "I was picking up this branch for my walking stick and found it was attached to something under the pile. I pulled and......I can't tell what that is under there."

Peshlakai cautiously approached. He'd been hiking and exploring rivers since he was a small child. Second nature to him. He looked at the mangled mess, analyzing the scene like a forensic scientist.

The stick seemed to be connected to something halfway in the earth. Horns. A skull, or a partial skull. He stood and was about to walk around the backside to get a comprehensive view of the situation when Sal reached to grab a stick from the pile.

The rattle from the snake broke the silence, followed by a quick strike toward Salvador's hand.

In that same moment Peshlakai was already reacting. He blocked Sal's arm, moving it up and away. The snakes' teeth missed digging into his flesh by inches.

Peshlakai instinctually grabbed Sal's arm as he was about to fall and moved him back several feet. Salvador's face turned white as a sheet.

"I think he likes you."

Peshlakai smiled and turned his attention back to the snake. He maneuvered the rattler onto his walking stick and carried it fifty feet away before releasing it. The snake slithered off into the distance.

Peshlakai returned to the pile and noticed the color had returned to Salvador's face. "Let's see what you found here Yogee."

Using his walking stick, Peshlakai began to gently move as much debris away from the skull as he could. He needed to get a good view of the specimen from every angle.

Next, he put his stick under the exposed base of the skull and slowly lifted it out of the earth, moving it several feet away from the pile before setting it back down on a patch of barren sand.

Satisfied that no more snakes were hidden in the pile, Peshlakai approached the skull, kneeling just inches away from one of the horns. Careful not to bump into the ancient spear head.

He looked up at Salvador and smiled. "Looks like a Native American weapon stuck into the skull of a buffalo."

Peshlakai continued to examine the specimen from every

angle. "One thing that's unusual is the size of the head and the length of the horns. Could be an extinct buffalo from an ancient kill, *bison antiquiss.*"

Peshlakai reached into an aged leather pouch strapped to his belt and pulled out a small brush. Carefully, he dusted off the dried mud, dirt and twigs from the buffalo skull. He turned it over and closely looked at the point of the spear in the skull.

"There's a few traders I know in Amarillo who'd be interested in this specimen. Big time collectors with deep pockets. If this is an ancient buffalo with a Folsom point attached, well…"

CHAPTER 55

They carried the buffalo skull to the truck and got back onto highway 287 north. Peshlakai turned on the radio.

"This is station 105.3FM, coming to you live from the Cotton Capital of Texas...spinnin' an old blues tune called DOWN IN TEXAS from Memphis's own legend, BLUES BOY WILLIE. This song is from his 2002 Album: BACK AGAIN, recorded on the Deep South label..."

Salvador looked over at Peshlakai while they drove through Memphis. He seemed distant, deep in thought. A crease of a smile slowly formed on his face as the old blues track echoed through the cab of the truck.

They passed the grain elevators and the football stadium with a sign displaying the teams' athletic achievements. CYCLONES. 2005 STATE CHAMPS.

They traversed the dusty town and were soon back out on the road where the land flattened on the horizon. Small clouds drifted slowly against a blue Texas sky.

Restless from the long drive, Sal unzipped his backpack and dug out his mom's box, looking carefully at each item.

According to the letter from his father, some were artifacts from ancient dig sites. There was also turquoise collected in Mexico and the Middle East, and other places from around the world.

Peshlakai glanced over at the specimens Salvador was holding. *Nice turquoise from an old collection. Mexican? Persian?*

"Interesting collection Yogee. Where'd you get it?"

"My mom gave me this box of stuff just before I left Dallas, with letters from my father who I never knew. He was studying to be an archeologist when she met him on vacation in Mexico when she was still a teenager."

Sal hesitated, feeling somewhat embarrassed about the rest of the story, although he didn't know why. "She only knew him for a week. I was an accident. He never knew about me. She didn't tell him."

Sal held up the bundle of letters.

"In these letters my father said that one of his ancestors was a Turkish trader who traveled through Europe during the early 1800's, trading turquoise and other archeological treasures. Even made a trip with some famous British explorers to the Yucatan Peninsula in Mexico."

Peshlakai looked at Salvador, smiled, and nodded his head. *"You probably got some of your old man in you."*

Salvador thought about that. Archaeology. Turquoise and artifacts. Traveling to remote places around the world. *Was it in his blood? Not sure. He was just trying to keep from being arrested.*

CHAPTER 56

The sun had turned orange, descending into the distant horizon on its daily pilgrimage across the sky. Streaks of soft blues and yellows painted the blue canvas of the plains.

Peshlakai gazed out the window, listening to the hum of the wheels on the asphalt. Feeling the energy of the land as the wind brushed against his skin.

He'd been traveling highway 287 since he was eighteen years old. Exploring the backroads, the rivers, the creeks. Canyons and rolling hills.

Salvador began to stir to life, having fallen asleep just past Clarendon.

"Are we in Amarillo yet?"

"Just passing through Goodnight. Getting close."

Peshlakai casually looked out the window and saw the shadow of the two-story ranch house that Colonel Charles Goodnight built in the late 1880's.

Goodnight, Texas. He'd often thought about this town. Goodnight represented an end and a beginning. The Comanche gave way to the cattleman. The buffalo was replaced by the cow.

It was a story about the old and the new. About what is, and what's becoming.

It was the story of America, and the story of history. Life keeps moving, changing. People have to adjust and adapt to survive.

PART FIVE

BUFFALO BURGER

CHAPTER 57

Evening lights lay twinkling along the distant horizon as they approached Amarillo. They passed the city limit sign, merged onto Interstate 40, and joined the flow of traffic headed west.

Peshlakai took an exit off I-40, continuing along the access road until he came to his destination. A restaurant with a forty-foot cowboy in neon lights.

He cruised through the parking lot several times until one of the cars in the front row pulled out. He wasted no time easing into the space.

Salvador stretched after he got out of the truck, casually looking around at the scene. There was a cow the size of an 18-wheeler, a windmill, and several flags above the building luring travelers off the highway.

They walked along the wood porch, into the restaurant and approached the hostess stand. "Two for dinner?"

"Yes", answered Peshlakai. "Could we sit in a booth by the front window?"

The hostess seated them quickly. Peshlakai looked out of

the window, wanting to make sure no one saw the buffalo skull in the truck bed. Or tried to enter the cab, where other items of value were stashed under the seat.

Sal looked through the menu. He was starving and everything looked good. "Peshlakai, ever had a buffalo burger?"

Peshlakai nodded. "Very lean, tasty. Good as any steak. Can't go wrong there."

A tall cowgirl walked up to the table, incredibly attractive. "Hi fellas. Ready to order?" She looked at Salvador confidently and smiled, fully aware of the effect she had on men.

She was young, maybe a year or two older than Sal. Wearing tight jeans that revealed a shapely figure, and a cowboy hat. Her long light brown hair bounced down her back, alive with its' own energy.

"I'll have the buffalo burger, mashed potatoes, green beans and a Coke."

She winked at Sal before turning her attention to Peshlakai.

"Cheeseburger, fries, cold slaw, and a coke. Separate checks please."

Before long their meal was served and both men attacked the food with a vengeance.

Peshlakai pulled out a small notebook and a pen and appeared to be documenting the events of the day. Or recording purchases and transactions. Could even be drawing.

Watching Peshlakai write reminded Sal of school. Did he miss it? Yea, kinda. Hated to admit it. "Suppose to graduate in a few weeks. Guess I'll never get my high school diploma now."

Peshlakai looked up from his writing, glanced out of the

window at his truck, then over to Salvador. He hesitated a few seconds before he spoke. "What have you learned since you left home?"

The question surprised Sal. He'd been on the run ever since he rode his bike into the Trinity Forest. Hadn't thought about what he'd learned.

Peshlakai smiled and thought of his own experience with education in high school. Sitting rigidly in a square desk, listening to a teacher talk on and on about things he had little interest in.

He looked at the young man across from him with a wisdom that only a lifetime of experience can give. *Salvador was unaware that he was in school, learning things that can't be taught in a classroom.*

A homeless drifter, he had the advantage of being out in the limitless sky of ideas. And experiences. Meeting people crisscrossing the continent from every part of the world. Learning about life the hard way. Painful lessons that allow for no excuses, only results.

CHAPTER 58

They paid for their dinner and walked out of the Big Texan Steakhouse. Peshlakai eased the truck out of the parking lot and down the I-40 access road.

"Yogee, welcome to stay with me tonight. I'll be dry camping, so you'll have to sleep in the bed of the truck. The campsite is safe, clean, and cheap. If that's not something you're interested in I can drop you off anywhere you want to go in Amarillo."

Sal's response was quick, having slept in a car half of his senior year. "Truck bed sounds good."

After a few miles they turned right, driving slowly down a narrow short road that led to the Big Texan RV-Campground.

They drove around the main office building and out to an area in the back where Peshlakai parked the truck. Walking over to the office, Peshlakai requested a camp space from the attendant on duty.

"Yes sir, we have one spot available. It'll be twenty dollars for dry camp or tent. That includes the use of showers, bathrooms, and pool. Free coffee and donuts in the morning." They walked out the back door and over to their space for the night.

Peshlakai opened the truck door and reached behind the seat. He pulled out a water-proof tarp and a blanket and handed them to Salvador. "You know where the bathroom is. Make sure you get your backpack. See you in the morning."

Salvador watched as Peshlakai situated himself in the cab of the pickup truck and fell asleep.

The RV park was crowded with big travel trailers. A few tents were set up close by. He situated the tarp and the blanket before laying down in the bed of the truck, then placed his backpack under his head for a pillow and stretched out.

The warm panhandle winds swept softly across the high plains, soothing his body after a long day of travel. Images of Samantha appeared in his mind. Her brown eyes, her warm smile, and the softness of her hand in his. Would he ever see her again?

He gazed at the sky above. *Wow! He'd never seen that many stars.*

Though relaxed, he had a hard time falling asleep. He tossed and turned, rubbing his back against the hard metal of the truck bed.

After what seemed like hours, he shut his eyes and began to dream wild dreams of rattlesnakes and riverbeds, policemen with guns drawn chasing him down the back alleys of an unknown city. And giant buffaloes walking across the highway.

He was abruptly awakened by the loud crack of thunder, followed by the pounding of heavy rain. Lifting his body from the bed of the truck, Sal looked out into the night. The sky was illuminated with great bolts of lightning, followed by the booming sound of thunder.

Then the hail came and crashed loudly against the metal of the truck. Sirens sounded in the distance, warning of a possible tornado.

Salvador placed the tarp partially over his head and looked into the bed of the truck. *Peshlakai was sound asleep*! He grabbed his backpack, the tarp and the blanket and sprinted over to a metal canopy that was connected to the main building.

Though soaking wet, he was at least protected against the direct contact of rain and hail and gale-force winds. Sal shivered, crouched his body into a ball, and wrapped himself in the tarp.

The storm continued for thirty minutes before losing its intensity. Finally, the clouds moved out and stars reappeared in the night sky. He leaned against the concrete office structure, closed his eyes, and drifted off into a deep sleep.

CHAPTER 59

The first thing he saw when he opened his eyes was Peshlakai sitting a short distance away on the bed of his pickup, drinking coffee and writing in his small notebook.

"Morning Yogee. Let's go get some breakfast."

Salvador felt the chill of the panhandle morning, amplified by the dampness of his clothes. Peeling the tarp away from his body, he entered the campground office, quickly showered and met Peshlakai at the truck.

Blue skies greeted them as they made their way onto I-40 west, joining the throngs of eighteen wheelers barreling down the interstate. It was only a few miles before Peshlakai exited off the freeway and parked his truck on the west side of the Cracker Barrel restaurant.

They entered and were seated by a window on the west side of the restaurant, at Peshlakai's request. He wanted an unobstructed view of his truck.

The waitress arrived almost immediately. "Coffee?"

"Please." Peshlakai turned toward Sal. "Yogee, breakfast is on me, since this might be our last meal together. I recommend the 'Smokehouse'."

"I'm down with that", Sal replied.

Peshlakai looked at Sal's appearance, and smiled. His hair was disheveled, and his clothes were wrinkled, damp, and dirty. He looked like what he was, a homeless drifter.

But as he took a sip of coffee, Peshlakai caught the image of a turquoise ring on Sal's left hand, a ring he was sure he'd never seen till today. "Nice ring Yogee. I hadn't noticed you wearing it. Mind if I look at it?"

Sal took off the ring and handed it to Peshlakai. It was the ring he'd traded for at Canton. "Yea, I thought I'd lost it until this morning. I was diggin' around in my backpack for my toothbrush, and I found it in a tiny compartment."

Peshlakai held the ring up to the light of the window and slowly examined it, running his fingers across the stone.

He took out a magnifying glass, looked on the inside of the ring, and was surprised to see the initials of a Navajo silversmith he knew from his boarding school days, decades ago.

For a full moment he found himself lost in the exquisite matrix of the turquoise, and the skill involved in the creation of the ring. It was a work of art. Reluctantly, he handed the ring back to Yogee, thinking about his friend he went to school with. And…about how quickly his life had passed by.

Deep in thought now, Peshlakai took a sip of the sacred cup, and remembered his first trip to Texas. Fresh out of high school and hungry for adventure.

"Came through Amarillo in 1960. I'd just graduated from high school, and the University of Texas offered me an athletic scholarship in track. I accepted the offer, but my heart wasn't into the discipline of the classroom. After a few months I packed my suitcase and took the bus back to the rez."

The waitress arrived, heat steaming off the sausage gravy and biscuits. She placed their breakfast on the table.

"Enjoy."

Methodically, they worked their way through the mountains of food: eggs, sausage, biscuits and groovy, hash brown potatoes, and grits.

After fifteen minutes the waitress reappeared and laid their ticket on the table. "No hurry gentlemen."

Memories continued to flood his mind, rolling back the years of his life. His sister's funeral. His son's death. And the unknown whereabouts of his grandson. A tear formed and made its way halfway down his cheek.

Peshlakai looked over at his young traveling companion and felt a deep compassion. Though in the prime of his life he was already homeless and running from the law. Hadn't even graduated from school.

"In 2005 my only son went to war in Iraq. Got killed by a road-side bomb in Fallujah. Left behind two kids and a wife." Peshlakai paused, allowing himself time to digest the words for the thousandth time.

Sal nodded quietly, sensing the heaviness that Peshlakai carried in his heart.

"His youngest son, Running Eagle, had a hard time with his father's death. Quit school early and lived on the road. Started drinking. He's been in and out of shelters and rehab facilities for the last ten years. Haven't seen him in a long time."

Peshlakai took a deep breath, wondering where his grandson might be now. Then, looking back across the table, he thought about Yogee. What would life throw at him next? Where would he end up? Like his grandson, the universe had redirected his path and he'd have to figure things out. He'd have to answer the question that every man has to answer.

"What's your plan now, Yogee?"

Sal shrugged. "Not sure. Been thinking about that myself." He picked up his coffee and looked out the window, watching the 18-wheelers traveling down the interstate. *Where was he going to sleep tonight? Were the police hot on his trail?*

Peshlakai had helped him get safely to Amarillo, but he would soon be gone, and Salvador would once again be on the run.

CHAPTER 60

Peshlakai got up from the table and looked down at Sal. "Meet you at the truck after I use the restroom."

Sal walked out to the truck and looked across the field at a large sign: T-ANCHOR FLEA MARKET. EXIT NOW.

Peshlakai approached the truck, opened the driver's side door and pulled out a map he'd picked up at the RV Campground. He walked to the front of the truck, tossed the map on the hood and opened it up.

"Yogee, I got a few places in Amarillo I need to go before I leave town. Welcome to ride along if you like. I can show you around so you can get a feel for the city, see if you want to stay."

He looked over at Peshlakai and nodded. Sounded like a good idea. It would give him some time 'til he had to make his next move.

Peshlakai took a few minutes and pointed out the major roads and highways before refolding the map and handing it to Sal. "The maps yours, might come in handy if you decide to stay."

Peshlakai pulled out of the parking lot and back onto the Interstate. Sal reopened the map and studied the layout of the city, noticing they were traveling east. He jotted down a few notes. The truck exited at the 335 Loop and headed north.

Within an hour they had circled the city and were back on the interstate, traveling west. Peshlakai exited north off the freeway and traveled into the heart of downtown Amarillo.

Veering right on Buchanan street they continued north, past a baseball park under construction. At Second Street they turned left and parked next to a building with a sign that read: FAITH CITY MISSION. A long line of homeless people waited by the door.

"My grandson stayed here several years ago. He called me, and I came to see him. Tried to get him to come back to the rez. He told me he wasn't ready. That was the last time I saw him."

Salvador's mind kicked into gear. Or was it his survival instincts. He could stay at the Big Texan RV Ranch for twenty dollars a night. Or stand in line at Faith City Mission and stay free, if the beds were not full. The other option, sleep on the streets.

Peshlakai circled the block and got back on Buchanan. Just past Amarillo Boulevard they connected to 287 North and exited onto the access road. They had traveled only a half a mile or so when suddenly…

'PING!!' *Sal jumped, startled by a golf ball bouncing off the truck.*

Peshlakai slowed the vehicle and looked to his right before pulling into a car lot on the east side of the 287 north access road, a big dent in his hood.

Out in the field by the car lot fence, a golfer stepped off a makeshift tee-box and walked toward the truck.

Six-foot two and wide at the shoulders, the golfer pulled his hat down on his head to shield the intensity of the sun. It was a friend Peshlakai hadn't seen in ten years. The man he'd bought his old Chevy truck from, and a golf legend in the panhandle, *TEXAS TIM.*

PART SIX

TEXAS TIM

CHAPTER 61

Tim smiled and tapped the handle of his golf club on the bed of the pickup. "Get that piece of junk off my lot."

Peshlakai got out and extended his hand. "Been a long time Tim. I see you're still working on your game."

"Yea. Got a semi-pro tournament in a few weeks. Be a lot of big-time players there trying to break into the majors. Golf pro I know called me, asked me to enter."

From the opposite entrance of the car lot a tricked-out '84 Ford short bed raced up to within six-inches of Texas Tim. "Where's Gunz?"

Sal looked curiously at the driver of the truck. He had a cigarette hanging out of his mouth as he talked, and another in his left hand. Both lit.

"Double-Cig, you may want to ease up on the gas when you roll in. He's over in *THE CAVE* getting ready for a fitness conference he's runnin' for a group of oil executives in Houston."

Double-Cig grinned. "Got a HOT lead! I need someone

to go with me on this one. Suppose to meet the guy at the Cattleman's Café in an hour."

From a small portable building next to Tim's office stepped a powerfully built man, flexing a twenty-pound dumbbell. His army-green cotton t-shirt exposed massive sculpted arms, large chest, and a thin waste. His hair was cropped close to his head, marine style.

"Suuuuup Double, ain't you got no training? No need to be racin' through the car lot. What chu got?"

The cigarette bounced up and down wildly in Double-Cig's mouth as he explained the car he'd found for sale.

"1967 Chevy Camaro SS, 327! Clear title. I've been working on this one for two years. The guy got in some trouble and needs money, quick. He's ready to unload it TO-DAY!"

Gunz carried the small twenty-pound barbell he had in his right hand and climbed into the truck with Double-Cig. "Texas, I'll try to bring this one home. Hard to find these '67's. It'll look good sitting on the lot. Later."

Double-Cigs right foot jammed the gas pedal to the floorboard and peeled ten feet of rubber as it screamed out of the parking lot.

Tim looked over at Peshlakai, smiled, and shook his head. "Crazy kid. Grew up at his uncle's salvage yard by Cactus, Texas. He lives, eats, breaths and drinks anything that has to do with old cars. No one in the city better at finding them."

Tim walked over to Peshlakai, then looked at Sal. "Who's this you're travelin' with?"

"Tim, this is Yogee", said Peshlakai, putting his hand on Sal's shoulder. "He's a friend of an awfully close friend of mine in Dallas who needed a ride to Amarillo. He'll be hanging around town a few days, thinking about his options. If nothing pops up for him in the next few days, he'll probably head west."

"Is that a fact?" said Tim, looking at Sal. He needed a lot man for about a month while Gunz was away. Someone young, strong, tough. And honest. Yogee wouldn't be with Peshlakai if he wasn't honest.

"Yogee, if you're looking for work, I need someone to help me out for about a month while Gunz is gone. Monday through Thursday, twelve hours a day, off on the weekends. We run a tight ship, but the pay is good. The job starts today. You interested?"

Salvador couldn't believe he was being offered a job on his first day in Amarillo.

"Yes sir, I'm interested," answered Sal, "but I got to be honest. I don't have a place to sleep tonight, I don't have transportation, and I don't know anything about the car business. Also, I got into some trouble with the police a few weeks ago."

Tim smiled and looked over at Peshlakai. "Sounds like you might be over-qualified for the position. Let's head over to the office and work out the details. I'll order us a couple of pizza's for lunch."

CHAPTER 62

Scott had been optimistic when he left Brendan Galloway at the Starbucks in Fort Worth two days ago. But his optimism was beginning to fade. He'd run into one dead end after another, trying to find out the name and location of the guy who was walking across the bridge with Leroy.

Famous now for rescuing a dog from the mouth of an alligator, Leroy's picture and story had been plastered in every major newspaper in the south.

But that wasn't the problem. The problem was nobody on the river or the market would answer questions, especially Leroy. If anyone knew, it would be Leroy.

Scott persevered and somehow dug up a few tidbits of information. Leroy's sidekick had only been in Fort Worth for a few days. Came from the Dallas area. Worked the Henderson Market on Sunday, then disappeared.

No name, no trace, no back story. Only the few pictures he'd taken.

Scott decided to head to Dallas for a few days. He'd beat the bushes and see if anything fell to the ground. If nothing materialized, he'd give up this temporary obsession and drift to another Texas town. Follow another story.

It was a warm spring afternoon when Scott pulled up to a local taqueria and ordered lunch. Sitting at one of the outdoor tables, he opened the newspaper and casually read through several articles before stumbling on a headline in the metro section. And there he was, a picture of the young man he was looking for. Salvador Jesus Gonzalez.

LOCAL HIGH SCHOOL STUDENT ARRESTED ON FELONY ASSAULT. NOW A FUGITIVE.

Scott put down his taco, pulled out a pen and underlined several details in the story. Salvador's age and ethnicity. His multiple fights in school. The high school he attended. The description of the assault. And the name of the reporter who wrote the article.

So, Salvador was in trouble with the law.

Climbing into his car, he pulled out the information he'd just written down, and listed the places he had to go to find out more about Salvador.

He felt the adrenaline pulsating through his body once again, a feeling he lived for, and one of the reasons he loved free-lance reporting. Now he was back in business and had to get down to the nitty-gritty work of investigation.

First stop, the police station.

CHAPTER 63

Tim picked up a slice of pepperoni pizza, took two bites and washed it down with a sixteen-ounce Coke. He needed to close the deal with Yogee, so he'd sweeten the pot.

"The pay is $100 dollars a day, four days a week. That's $1600 a month. Includes breakfast and lunch. Rent for staying at the car lot is $200 a week, $800 for the month. How's that sound?"

Considering he might have been sleeping on the street tonight the offer sounded great. "Sounds fair Tim. Do you know where I'll be sleeping?"

Texas Tim looked at Yogee, uncertain how to answer. But Tim was always quick on his feet when the situation demanded it. "Sure. Let's go out on the lot and I'll show you."

He looked around the car lot for some sleeping options for his new employee. There were three buildings on site: the OFFICE, the CAVE, and the STUDIO. Those were all off-limits for overnight guests.

Walking around to the south side of the building Tim stopped dead in his tracks. There it was, a vehicle that came in yesterday he'd forgotten about.

"Here it is Yogee, your new home. A twenty-seven-foot 1966 Dodge Traveco RV. I bought it from a friend who needed to get it off his property. Water and electric don't work, and the motors not running. Might need some cleaning."

Texas Tim unlocked the door and let Salvador take a look. He climbed the two stairs and entered. Looked like a cyclone hit.

Piles of worn and stained clothes lay everywhere. Broken pieces of wood, empty sacks of fast food and unfinished cokes covered the kitchen area. Along with hundreds of dead bugs and cigarette butts.

He walked back to the bathroom, looked in, and quickly closed the door. Not sure what that smell was.

But the place was enclosed and would protect him from the wind and the rain. And it was a lot bigger than his 1962 Chevy wagon, and a lot dryer and safer than the back of Peshlakai's pickup.

It might need a little fixing up, but he'd have plenty of time for that. And, his new home was completely self-contained with a bathroom, kitchen, closets, chest of drawers, and a bed.

"How much did you say the rent is per month?"

"$800."

Sal calculated the amount of money he had in his backpack from the sale of the old rifle, and the money he'd gotten from Mr. T and Troy. "I'm interested, but it looks like I might be cleaning the place for weeks. And fixing the appliances. Most I can pay in rent is $400."

Salvador surprised himself with the authority in his voice in making the offer. Must have picked up a few things watching Samantha. Or hanging out with Leroy and Paleo at

Traders Village.

But to Texas Tim this was all normal, just like sleeping or breathing. Make an offer on a unit. Counteroffer. Counter-counter offer. It's what happened in the marketplace.

"Yogee, that's a generous offer, but I can't take less than $600." Tim smiled. He was having fun now.

Sal reached into his money belt and pulled out $450 cash, laying it on the console next to the driver's seat.

"I'll make it $450."

Cash offer on the table. Texas Tim's response was quick from decades of experience. Time to wrap up the deal. "Come up to $500 and we'll close the deal."

Fresh from the memory of sleeping through a thunderstorm in the back of a pickup the night before, Sal eagerly accepted the deal. They shook hands, exited the TRAVECO and walked back to the office.

After strolling the car lot, Peshlakai rejoined Tim and Sal. "Peshlakai, how long you staying in Amarillo?"

"Leaving town either tonight or tomorrow morning after I tie up a few loose ends. If you don't mind, I'd like to take Yogee with me. I can have him back later this afternoon."

"No problem. Gunz should be back by then to show Yogee what needs to be done on the lot. But before you go there's something you will be interested in. It's about your grandson."

Peshlakai's face became animated. He'd heard his grandson might be in Texas, but he had no idea where. Texas was a big state.

"He's working for a friend of mine I've done business with for decades. They showed up together one day about six months ago. After that, they made it a habit to stop in to see what trades I got, and what other items I may have taken in as part of a down payment on a vehicle."

205

Tim reached in the top left drawer of his desk and pulled out a golf score card from Ross Rogers Golf Course. He handed it to Peshlakai.

The front of the card displayed the names of two players, and their score for 18-holes: *TEXAS TIM, 68. RUNNING EAGLE, 79.* On the back was a hand drawn map. *"These are the directions that'll take you right to his place."*

Peshlakai stared at the map for several minutes, tears forming in his eyes.

CHAPTER 64

Energized by the news of his grandson, Peshlakai sped south on 287 till they got to I-40. They exited on Grand Avenue and eased on to the access road west.

Just past the Cracker Barrel restaurant, Peshlakai turned north on a side road between two hotels and parked in front of a big sign: T-ANCHOR FLEA MARKET.

"Yogee, this is it. Looks like he's living in a clump of trees behind the flea market. I think that's his tent. Wait here. I'll be back in a minute."

Peshlakai exited the truck and followed a dirt path, leading him down an embankment next to a small body of water. He continued on until he came upon a grill surrounded by folding chairs. A beat-up metal coffee pot, steam rising out of the spout, was sitting on a rock above a small pit fire, just a few feet away from a canvas tent.

The flap of the tent abruptly opened and a powerfully built young Native American male walked up to Peshlakai until they were face to face. It was his 29-year-old grandson, Running Eagle. A tear trickled down his weathered face.

Running Eagle had left the rez after his senior year in high school. Addicted to the bottle, he'd been unable to shake the negative effects of the memory of his hero father who'd died in Iraq when he was 16-years old.

Peshlakai's eyes were now flooded. He stepped forward and embraced his grandson. Running Eagle buried his face in his grandfathers' chest and wept. After several minutes, Running Eagle pushed away and looked Peshlakai directly in the eyes.

"Grandfather…I've shamed our family name for years, that's why I couldn't come home. But I'm clean now. Gave up drinking two years ago after I got out of prison. Moved back to Amarillo and rebuilt my life."

Peshlakai looked back at Salvador, waved him over, then followed his grandson to the chairs surrounding the fire.

Running Eagle looked up as Sal approached the camp site. Peshlakai introduced him. "Friend of Paleo's. Name's Yogee. Needed a ride to Amarillo, so he's been travelin' with me the past few days."

Running Eagle looked at Sal and nodded. *Yogee. Not a bad road name. How many road names had he created since he left the Rez?*

"Yogee, nice to meet you. Welcome to my campsite. Hope you like the coffee." He pulled two cups out of a portable cooler, filled them with coffee, and handed them to his guest.

Running Eagle stood, picked up a golf club laying by the side of his tent, and motioned his guests to follow him. "Grandfather, I've got to show you something I've been working on for the past few months."

He led them down the embankment a few feet before angling north. Then walked a short distance to a much larger tent located in a small cluster of trees at the back of the flea market.

They walked up to the tent, which was twice the size of Running Eagles, and entered. They were unprepared for what they saw.

CHAPTER 65

Before them was an open-dirt pit that measured four-foot wide, six-foot long, and three feet deep, exposing what seemed to be pre-historic dinosaur bones.

Peshlakai was surprised, and curious. "You're working at a dinosaur excavation site?"

Running Eagle smiled and nodded.

"Correction grandfather. I'm the DISCOVERER...of a dinosaur site. And, I'm the designated paleontologist-in-training through a local university. Officially, it's called the T-ANCHOR MAMMOTH SITE. I stumbled upon them one Saturday morning in late February after two days of heavy rain."

Running Eagle continued. "I showed a few of the bones to my boss. He said they were dinosaur bones, but he wasn't sure what type. That night we met up with a noted paleontologist who'd been writing a professional paper about the 1929 Mammoth excavation under the Santa Fe building in downtown Amarillo."

"The paleontologist identified them, gave a legal

description, and we began an official excavation. So far we've uncovered a Columbian Mammoth, a camel, and a tooth from a saber-tooth cat."

From outside the tent the sound of a police siren filled the air. Sal's heart skipped a beat.

They exited the dig site and walked back to the fire. Running Eagle continued on at a brisk pace, past Peshlakai's truck and over to the approaching police car. For several minutes Running Eagle and the policeman had a conversation. When it was over, the policeman rolled up his window and drove away. Running Eagle strolled casually back to his tent.

"That was Officer Smith, friend of mine. He was checking to see whose truck was parked by my camp site. This is his beat and he keeps an eye on the place."

Running Eagle noticed the fear in Sal's eyes and wondered what he was running from. But It didn't matter. He was with his grandfather, who could judge the character of men better than anyone he knew.

"How long you stayin' in Amarillo Yogee?"

Sal looked over at Peshlakai, who nodded. That meant go ahead, tell him the truth. "Not sure. Got in a little trouble a few days ago. Trying to keep a low profile."

Running Eagle nodded and smiled. He knew what it was like to be on the run.

"Yogee, if you're looking for work my boss needs someone to help us at the flea market on the weekends. Right now it's just him and me. We need one more person who's honest, someone we can trust. You wouldn't be with my grandfather if you weren't honest."

Running Eagle continued. "Your first day would be this Saturday, if you're interested. We start setting up at seven. He pays in cash, $100 a day."

Salvador couldn't believe his luck. Two job offers on his first day in Amarillo. And a place to sleep. He wasn't sure how he'd get to the market at seven on Saturday, but he'd figure it out.

He looked down at the old silver bracelet on his wrist and brushed his hand across the weathered stone.

CHAPTER 66

The rest of the day was a blur. Peshlakai took Sal to What-A-Burger for an early dinner, then to Walmart to help him stock up his for his RV-home. They filled up their grocery cart with Beanie-Weenies, chips, bedding, and a case of bottled water. In addition, they bought a bicycle, some toiletries, and a cheap notebook.

They arrived back at the car lot just before it was about to close and unloaded the items. Tim finished waiting on a customer, then walked over to the RV.

"Sal, Gunz got tied up with some business so he won't be here until tomorrow morning. He'll show you how to open the lot. Here's an extra-key to the bathroom, and over by the tool shed there's an outdoor water spicket. Lock the gate when Peshlakai leaves. Manana."

Tim hopped on his Harley and rode away.

Peshlakai helped Sal put the rest of his meager belongings into the RV and walked over to his truck. "I'll stop by tomorrow before I head out. Night Yogee."

Sal climbed up into the 66 Dodge Traveco and sat in the

driver's seat, mesmerized by the changing colors of the sunset. He attempted to recall the things that had happened since he left home. The endless new environments, the people, the experiences.

Darkness blanketed the night sky, and his eyes became heavy.

He climbed over the piles of discarded trash and dirty clothes that were strewn on the floor of his new home, then stretched out on the bed. From habit he grabbed his backpack and laid it by his side.

In no time at all he was asleep.

CHAPTER 67

Gunz arrived at 5:30 am, his usual time. Unlocking the gate, he scanned the car lot for anything unusual or out of place.

Through the years, life had taught him to be careful. Take nothing for granted. And to work hard every day. Got to produce, add value to the people around you. Your family, your friends, your employer. It'd been drilled into him by his father from the time he was five-years old. That was thirty years ago.

He walked over to the office and was about to unlock the door when he noticed a note on the window from Tim.

'That drifter kid I hired is staying in the '66 Traveco. Goes by the name YOGEE. He starts work today at 6 am. Green as they come but seems willing to work. Give him the TREATMENT…so we can see what he's made of. TT.'

Gunz smiled at the thought of training a green horn. He walked over to the RV and slammed his hand forcefully against the back of the Traveco where the bed was located.

BAM! BAM! BAM! "Wake up Cinderella. Showtime!"

Salvador shot up, looked around the RV and noticed several roaches scampering across his bed. He rushed down the small hallway and tripped on his shoes, falling face first to the floor. Pushing himself up, he opened the door and looked out onto the car lot.

"Six bells baby, time to GET DOWN! We got some units to move, so get that skirt off and get your driftin' ass down here!"

Sal tensed up but moved quickly to find his shoes and socks. *This guy looked serious.* Frantically he tied his shoes and stepped down onto the asphalt pavement. "I'm ready Mr. Gunz."

Gunz looked at Sal, disgusted. Hair messed up, nose bleeding, shirt and pants wrinkled and dirty. And it smelled like he hadn't showered in a week.

"This ain't no homeless shelter son, it's a business. One of the top car dealerships in the Texas panhandle. Tomorrow morning make sure you're showered and have clean clothes on before you come to work. And get a haircut!"

Gunz shoved a pair of clean but worn overalls into Sal's chest and walked quickly toward the entrance gate of the car lot. Sal ran to keep up.

When they arrived at the gate, Gunz flipped out an index card and handed it to Sal. The card was entitled: 7 FUNDAMENTALS OF OPENING A CAR LOT.

"Master the FUN-DA-MEN-TALS. That's the name of the game. Figure out the basics and master those." He looked at Sal, seeing if he was taking in the information.

"Same thing in running a car lot successfully. Master the fundamentals of the business. And do it right every day, without someone having to stand over you. I AIN'T YO MAMA!" Gunz paused, wanting his words to sink in.

"In your case, we only want you to master the 7 fundamentals. Any questions?"

Sal read through the seven steps on the card. "No sir."

Gunz nodded. "Good. First, I'm going to *TELL* you how it's done. Next, I'm going to *SHOW* you how it's done. Then I'm going to *INVOLVE* you in the process of how it's done until you have it perfected. No short cuts. Let's start."

Salvador followed Gunz around all day, listening to his instructions, watching how he performed the tasks and diving into whatever was asked of him.

His mind was spinning with all the information dumped into his brain in a short span of time, but he was determined to do things the right way. He would master the fundamentals.

Tim arrived about nine in the morning and practiced his golf swing before doing some work in the office. He came in and out throughout the day. Sold two cars, took in six car payments, and ate lunch with Gunz and Sal.

By 4:00 pm they'd finished all the chores and sat down on the bed of one of the car lot pickup trucks with a plate of BBQ from Wesley's Bean Pot. Gunz was shoveling it in and talking.

"Good job today Yogee. How's that BBQ?"

Sal's mouth was full as he tried to answer. "Rery rood."

"I'm leaving Friday for Houston, so I'll only be training you for two more days. You work like you did today and you'll have it down. Any questions while I'm gone, just ask Tim."

Gunz left, so Tim and Sal began to close the lot. "Yogee, come on into the office so we can talk."

Sal followed Tim into the office, exhausted.

Tim picked up his putter and began practicing on the office putting green area where customers could *'PUTT FOR THE GREEN'*. Make four out of four putts, price of the car goes down by $400. Three out of four, $300. And so on.

Tim leaned the putter against the wall and sat at his desk, facing Sal. "Gunz said you did a good job today. We appreciate that. But the secret, if you can call it that, is to do a good job every day. It's like golf. Good grip, good stance, good swing. Good golfers do it right every day."

Tim walked over to Sal and slapped him on the back. "Follow me to the gate and lock it up after I leave. I got to get over to Ross Rogers and get nine holes in before it gets dark."

Sal followed Texas Tim out of the office and watched him drive off before locking the gate.

He walked over to the Traveco, entered, and grabbed a bottled water. Stepping outside, he meandered slowly around the car lot, listening to the words of Gunz as they echoed in his mind.

'Turn-key ready. When a customer gets in a car, they want it clean and running. Hit the key, and the car starts purring. Probably the biggest part of the sale, and the most important of the fundamentals.'

Though exhausted in mind and body from ten hours of intense work, he felt a sense of contentment and accomplishment.

Gunz pushed him hard, but he didn't mind. He was used to life being hard. He'd learned a long time ago to deal with whatever came his way, without complaining.

Sal entered his new home and switched the tent lamp on.

Several roaches scampered across the kitchen counter before disappearing into the wall. Trash, worn out clothes and cigarette butts were everywhere, mixed in with remnants of fast food sacks. Half-filled plastic bottles lined the floor by the bathroom. The stench of something dead filled the air, along with other unfamiliar smells.

Friday. My one day off. I gotta get this place clean.

CHAPTER 68

Friday found Sal sleeping soundly till awakened by a tingling on the top of his foot. He lifted his head and looked toward the end of the bed. *A large mouse was nibbling on his big toe.*

He jerked his leg wildly, jumped off the bed and scraped his arm against the narrow hallway wall. It took a minute for him to calm down and think clearly. Friday, his one day off. He'd shower, clean out the Traveco, then take a bike ride through the hood.

It was dark when Sal exited the RV to take his morning shower. With the water running he looked up into the sky to find the Scorpio constellation. *There it is. Must be about 4 am.*

Back inside, he got to work. He filled four large trash bags and scrubbed every inch of the place before taking a short break. While resting, he looked around the empty living area. He didn't need much, maybe an end table and a few chairs. And a small kitchen table.

Sal walked over to the car lot office and, using the keys Gunz had left with him, opened the front door. By habit he performed the 7 fundamentals: coffee on, bathroom cleaned, car keys placed on pegs by Tim's desk, and so on.

Once the coffee was ready, he filled his cup and took it back to the RV. The only seat available was the drivers captain chair.

He grabbed his backpack, climbed into the seat, and looked out the front window of the vehicle. Early morning light displayed soft blues in the sky. He took a deep breath and slowly exhaled. Followed by a sip of coffee.

Finally, he had his own place. This was the first time since he'd left home that he had a few minutes to catch his breath.

Being his only day off, he decided to make the best of it. *Backpack. I need to go through my backpack and get it organized.* And maybe write an entry into my journal, like Peshlakai.

Sal pulled out his journal and wrote an abbreviated account of the things he'd experienced since he left home. The man he beat. The police interrogation. And his decision to become a fugitive.

He detailed his travels through the Great Trinity Forest, the ride down the river, his movement through the markets in Dallas and Fort Worth. And his drift north on highway 287.

Putting his pen down, he placed his journal in his backpack and wondered where he would end up. *Would the police eventually catch him and put him in jail? Or would he be running for months, maybe years, hiding out in the wide-open spaces of the Southwest?*

****

Peshlakai pulled his truck into the car lot just before noon, his arm on the drivers' side window ledge. "What's that you're grilling Tim?"

Tim looked up from the grill. "Wisconsin brats boiled in

beer and onions. Got mustard, pickles and sauerkraut to put on it. Let me get you a plate."

Peshlakai climbed out of his truck and walked over to Tim. "Decided I'd stay a few extra days and hang out with my grandson. How's Yogee doing?"

"That kids a worker! He had the Traveco cleaned and organized by the time I opened this morning. He also had everything at the lot ready for the day, something he didn't have to do."

As they were talking Salvador opened the front door of his RV and looked out onto the car lot, coffee in hand.

Peshlakai walked back to his truck, picked up the book *Empire of the Summer Moon*, and headed over to the RV. "Morning Yogee. Here's that book you were reading when we rode into town. I finished reading it last night and thought you might want it for your library."

"Thanks. Don't have a library yet, but I do want to know more about Quanah Parker."

Peshlakai nodded. "How's RV living?"

"Come on in and take a look."

Peshlakai stepped into the Traveco and walked through. Clean. Organized. Just needs a few chairs and a table. And a small bookshelf.

As he was turning to speak, he bumped into Salvador's outstretched hand that concealed a gift. "It's for you Peshlakai, a small thank you for all you've done for me."

Peshlakai smiled and reached out to receive the gift. It was the ring he examined at Cracker Barrel a few days ago. He hesitated before accepting the gift.

"Yogee…this ring might be worth a little money. It's from a well-known silversmith whose work is highly desired."

"Well, now it's yours. Least I can do for all your help."

Peshlakai took the ring and carefully placed it on his finger. He was deeply moved. "Place looks nice, just needs a few pieces of furniture. What do you say we go hit some garage sales, see what we can find?"

"That'll work."

Peshlakai looked at the ring on his finger as he drove out of the car lot, captivated by the dark black matrix engrained in the blue stone. Made by one of his friends in boarding school over sixty-years ago.

He knew Yogee hadn't heard about the fame of the silversmith. Nor did he know anything about the value of the stone.

PART SEVEN

TASCOSA

CHAPTER 69

For some reason Tascosa rarely forgot historical facts. His teachers said he had a photographic memory. One fact he remembered well was November 22, 1963. It was the day that John F. Kennedy was assassinated in Dallas, Texas.

But that date was seared into his consciousness for another reason. It was the same day his mom walked him to a Greyhound bus station in a small town outside Lubbock, Texas and dropped him off at the terminal. He was seven years old.

In his right hand was a one-way bus ticket, and around his neck was a sign that read: PLEASE DELIVER TO BOYS RANCH, TEXAS.

At the time, it was the worst thing that had ever happened to him. Yes, they were dirt poor, all eight of them. His six brothers and sisters, and his mom. Yes, they lived in an abandoned box car on the outskirts of town and never had enough food to eat. But it was his family that he was leaving, and he cried and cried as he sat at the station.

Something died in him that day on the long ride through

the open plains of the Texas Panhandle, traveling to an unfamiliar place along the banks of the Canadian River.

But little did he know that the same bus taking him away from all he'd known and loved was also taking him toward his destiny.

****

Sixty-two-year old Tascosa loaded the last of his merchandise into the back of his van, stopping for a moment to look out at the morning sun as it rose along the eastern horizon of the high plains.

The seven acres he owned on the outskirts of Amarillo had a great view of the landscape. Beautiful sunrises and colorful sunsets. He never tired of it.

He stepped off the front porch of his 1200 square foot adobe ranch house and walked over to the outdoor stone oven he'd built decades ago.

The oven was the centerpiece of his ranch, connecting the rustic adobe with his blacksmith-silversmith shop he'd built inside the shell of a 1950 Santa Fe train car.

He poured himself a cup of coffee and sat on a stump just a few feet away, thinking back to a decision he made at the age of twenty-five.

The year, 1982.

He'd been out of high school for seven years and had spent that time working in construction, factories and small ranches. And though he enjoyed the work, he felt that something was not quite right, that his life was adrift. He was unhappy, restless, and deeply in debt.

That's when an idea came to him late one night, sitting around a campfire in the Palo Duro Canyon. It was an idea

225

that'd been slowly building for years, buried somewhere deep inside his subconscious.

Sell everything you own. Take the cash, buy an old truck and some camping gear. Do what you've wanted to do since you first arrived at Boys Ranch at the age of seven. Explore the Texas Panhandle, the Canadian River, and the old wild west town of Tascosa.

At first, he was afraid to talk to people about it. Afraid his friends and co-workers wouldn't understand him. Afraid they would criticize him. Tell him to grow up and accept responsibility.

But the idea stayed in his mind. Seeped into his soul.

He woke up one morning in late spring of 1982 and made the decision. Sold all his belongings, turned in his new truck, bought a beat-up Ford F-100 and followed the drifter's trail.

That trail took him on a wild journey along the Canadian River Valley that the early explorers had traveled in the 1800's.

He camped on the open caprocks of the Llano Estacado and underneath the cottonwood trees along the small creeks and tributaries of the river. He visited every town on the high plains, rummaged through every museum.

He found ancient native American trails and documented paleontology sites along the length and breadth of the Texas Panhandle.

And all the while he studied books. Books on the history of the high plains. Biographies of heroes and outlaws, European explorers and Native Americans. He read westerns, he traveled, he documented.

After a year he returned to Amarillo with a knowledge about the Texas panhandle that few had.

He also discovered something about himself, a discovery that would become the theme of his career. *History.* It was history that fascinated him. *And old things. Things that were worn, broken down, soulful. Things that had a story.*

This discovery led him to the antique stores on old Route 66, where he landed a job as a store clerk. Within months he become one of the antique dealers at the store.

After two years on sixth street he felt restless again and decided to strike out on his own. Start his own business. He was learning to trust his instincts.

He confided in his boss about his upcoming career move. If anyone would understand his dream, it would be his boss. *'You want to make a career out of trading antiques at the local flea market? All they sell is used junk, and nobody makes money. You'll go broke in six months.'*

But he'd run the numbers a dozen times and was confident he could make it work. It turned out to be the best decision of his life.

CHAPTER 70

Sal woke Saturday morning in the predawn hours, flipped on his tent lamp in the RV and laid out his clothes.

Gunz had trained him relentlessly for three days, repeating the mantra of fundamentals until he performed them in his sleep.

He looked around the trailer. 1950's retro kitchen table, two chairs and a small shelf that held the only four books he owned. A half-filled coffee cup from the day before sat on the counter. *Reilly's Luck* by his bed, next to his journal.

He grabbed his towel and a bar of soap, walked outside and over to a pole by the tool shed with a hose attached six feet high and took a nice cold shower. Returning to the trailer, he dressed, strapped on his backpack and exited the Traveco.

Making sure the car lot gate was locked, he jumped on his bike and rode through the field, following Buchanan street to the heart of the city. He passed several small groups of homeless people before turning left on 3rd, then north on Ross 'til he ran into the T-ANCHOR FLEA MARKET.

It's a tiny market, he thought. Only one building, seven

outdoor canopies and a few open-air spaces. Sal pulled into the small outdoor flea market area and rode around looking for the location of their set up. F-25, 26. Underneath a canopy by the back fence.

As he approached, he noticed Running Eagle standing next to a small, older man who was actively engaged in negotiations over items that were stacked on the table. Sal leaned his bike against the nearby fence and walked over to the action.

Running Eagle stopped momentarily. "Morning Yogee. Coffee's over here to my right, box of Dunkin Donuts next to it. Help yourself."

Sal picked up an empty cup, filled it, and grabbed a donut.

A massive farmer wearing overalls and a John Deere hat picked up a pair of antique spurs and placed them in a pile he'd made.

"Tascosa, you and I been doing business for pert-near thirty years. Give me your best price."

Tascosa barely made an expression, just a small nod of his head. He picked up each item in the pile, looked them over intently, and slowly raised his head to face the fellow trader. His voice was soft as he spoke, his disposition calm.

"Hank, 'preciate your business. These seven items you selected are all fresh finds from across the panhandle, and you're the first one to see them."

Tascosa casually picked up the pieces as he spoke.

"Two Spanish Colonial spurs, a rusted out French Musket found in the Canadian River, three Triassic specimens and a metal gasoline sign from the 1950's. My price for the pile is $1,650."

The tall man hesitated several seconds before making a counteroffer. "Think you can let 'em go for $1,200?"

Tascosa casually looked down at the pile and repeated the procedure, picking up each piece, looking it over intently, then placing it back on the table.

"That's a reasonable offer Hank, but the best I can do today is $1,500."

Hank nodded, reached into his pocket and put the money on the table. He knew these were valuable items that he could easily double or triple his money on.

He also knew there were antique dealers from 6th Street in line behind him, personal friends of Tascosa who would quickly pick up the items he selected and pay whatever price quoted.

"Thanks Hank. Always a pleasure. Running Eagle, take over for me while I warm up my coffee." Tascosa poured himself a cup, took a bite from a chocolate éclair and walked over to Sal.

"Morning Yogee. Running Eagle's told me all about you. Glad to have you with us today. Name's Tascosa. Just hang out with us for the next few hours and watch. It's a small market, but there's a lot of action behind the scenes."

Tascosa took a sip and continued. "After lunch, Running Eagle's going to take you to the Panhandle Plains Museum, followed by a night of camping in the Palo Duro Canyon. It's the first thing I do with all my new employees. It'll give you a big advantage in understanding our business here. What we buy, sell, or trade for."

He walked over to the donut table, sat his coffee down, then returned to Sal. "Now, let's look at that buffalo skull you found in the Prairie Dog Town Fork of the Red."

Tascosa reached under a corner table and pulled out the skull Sal had uncovered in the river. Picking it up carefully, he displayed it on a table.

"Peshlakai came by my ranch two days ago and showed me the skull. It's a rare specimen, very rare. Only seen two in my thirty-seven-years of trading. We took it to three reputable collectors with deep pockets. Got three cash offers."

Tascosa took out three index cards and laid them on the table. Each had a name, phone number, and a cash offer clearly written. *All were above $8,000.*

"Any of these offers interest you?"

CHAPTER 71

Sal stared at the cash offers in front of him and was about to respond when an old man reached across the table and tapped Tascosa on the shoulder.

"You buyin' old cigarette lighters today Tascosa?"

Tascosa looked up and smiled. It was his long-time picker, Uncle Zippo. They'd been doing business together from the beginning.

"Happy to look. What'da ya got?"

Uncle Zippo reached into his front pocket, pulled out an old cigarette lighter and handed it to Tascosa.

"It's a 3-barrell Zippo from the 1930's, mint condition. Take $300 for it."

Tascosa flipped the top of the lighter open, pulled out a small paper note from the empty chamber and closed it. This was a ritual they'd perfected over the years.

Unfolding the paper, he read through the hand scribbled note before discretely placing it into his pocket.

"I'll take it Uncle Zip. Let's go over to the van." Uncle Zippo followed Tascosa to the passenger side of the van where the two engaged in hushed discussions.

"Tascosa, there's a dealer in the 6th Street Antique Mall that found a trunk in the attic of a condemned house. That thang's filled with hand-drawn maps, letters, receipts, and artifacts from old *Rag Town City, the first community of people in Amarillo.*"

Tascosa nodded thoughtfully. He'd read a lot of articles about old Rag Town City...stories about the saloons, gambling halls and whorehouses that serviced the railroad workers in the late 1800's.

Uncle Zippo looked around, then leaned in closer. *"The dealer said there's a detailed map, with the exact location of the legendary CASNER GOLD from 1876.* He wants to meet you for lunch tomorrow at the Golden Light Café on Route 66."

Tascosa quickly pulled $300 out of his pocket and handed it to Uncle Zippo. "Tell him I'll be there." He started to head back to the table before abruptly turning around to face Uncle Zippo.

"By the way Zip, we're having dinner at the ranch tomorrow at 6. Texas Tim's mom is makin' a pot of pinto beans with ham hocks, and two skillets of cornbread. I'm smoking a brisket tonight. Like you to come if you can."

Uncle Zippo nodded. "Put me on the list. Ain't never turned down beans and fresh made skillet cornbread."

Tascosa opened the note and read through it again before flipping it over to the back. He'd been looking in that area for decades for a box that had been rumored to be buried during the boom days of the Texas panhandle. One-foot wide, two-foot long, one-foot deep. *Wrapped in a gunny sack and filled with gold coins.*

Legend had it that two gold miners from New Mexico, the Casner Brothers, moved to the panhandle in 1876, buried

$20,000 in gold coins, and were murdered by some outlaws. To date, no one had discovered the gold.

He'd heard about these buried gold coins ever since he arrived at Boys Ranch. It was only one of many legendary stories that had lived in his mind for 55 years.

Tascosa gently folded the note and placed it deep into his pocket.

CHAPTER 72

Sierra's long, sandy-blond hair danced in the wind as she slowed her horse to a trot, then a slow walk. She guided him along the shore of the Canadian River and looked out at their family's ranch.

They'd inherited the 640 acres from her father's grandfather, who'd purchased the land for almost nothing during the 1920's.

Looking out at the caprocks and rolling hills, Sierra felt an array of conflicting emotions.

Her life in the wide-open spaces of the Texas panhandle seemed to be coming to an end. Last week she'd graduated from college with a master's degree in Athletic Training and had a job offer from a prestigious four-year university.

Though her life in high school and college had revolved around academics and golf, her heart was with the land. Hiking along the Canadian River. Exploring the arroyos, the buttes and the canyons. And collecting dinosaur bones and artifacts with her father since she was a little girl.

Another thing that weighed on her mind was the attention

she was getting from two professional men. Both were pursuing her aggressively. One was a local oil executive. The other, a senior vice-president of the largest bank in north Texas.

Though flattered by their attention, Sierra was fiercely independent and belonged to no one. She'd followed her own path her entire life, seeking counsel only from her father.

"Sierra, time to go. We've got to stop by Wesley's on the way into Amarillo and pick up some BBQ."

They climbed into her father's quad-cab Ford pickup and traveled south to Amarillo. As they entered the city, they made a quick stop at Wesley's to pick up their order.

"You going to take that job at the University of Texas?"

"I don't know dad. Seems like a great opportunity. I'm gonna' hang out at the ranch a few days and think about it."

After passing through the downtown area her father eased the truck onto I-40 east, exiting at Ross. He traveled north for about a mile before pulling into the T-Anchor Flea Market.

Sierra grabbed the sack of lunches they'd picked up and walked with her father to the outdoor market.

Rex, Sierra's father, approached Tascosa, right arm outstretched. "Morning Tascosa. We stopped at Wesley's and got a few combination BBQ plates for you and your helpers."

"You didn't have to bring us lunch Rex, but you know we can't turn down Wesley's. Sierra, can you take two plates over to the boys while I mind the store?"

Sierra walked over and gave Tascosa a hug. "I've missed seeing you on the weekends. Guess I've been spending all my time trying to finish school. Where are the boys?"

"Out back by the playa lake, working on the excavation site. One of them lives in a tent by the mammoth he discovered. He's been with me a while. Surprised you don't know him. The other one started today, a drifter kid from Dallas. Not sure how long he'll be here."

Sierra nodded. "Dad told me about the bones you found, that's why I came this morning. I wanted to see it with my own eyes."

Sierra picked up two plates of food and walked back to the playa lake, looking for the mammoth excavation site. She passed the blue tent where Running Eagle lived, noticing steam rising from a coffee pot on top of an outdoor camp stove.

She continued past the tent until she came to a sign in front of the larger tent: TEXAS HISTORICAL SOCIETY EXCAVATION SITE: NO TRESPASSING. VIOLATORS WILL BE PROSECUTED.

Without hesitation she bent down and eased into the tent, carrying the two plates of BBQ. She looked around the room, spellbound.

In front of her were two young men, standing over a scattered collection of bones, talking about the height of the mammoth and the length of his tusk.

She'd been interested in dinosaur bones her whole life, but that's not what captured her attention. It was the boy with the bronze skin and the long black hair.

Sal caught movement out of the corner of his eyes and turned toward the entrance. An attractive young female had entered the tent and was standing there, starring at Running Eagle.

Running Eagle noticed Sal look away and turned toward the entrance. A young woman was standing there, looking at him. He took a deep breath and straightened his back. "Hi."

Sierra returned a nervous smile and looked into his eyes, drawn by a mysterious magnetic force that captivated her.

Something exotic, ancient, intoxicating. *What had she stumbled upon?*

CHAPTER 73

From the bottom of Palo Duro Canyon, Running Eagle walked over to a stack of wood at the edge of their campsite and picked up a few pieces to add to the dwindling flame.

"You took in a lot of information at the Panhandle Plains Museum today Yogee. 14,000 years of human history, and 600 million years of earth's history. Not to mention the five miles of hiking we did after dinner."

Salvador grabbed a rock he'd found in the creek bed and lifted it up to the fire light. "What did you say this one's called?"

"Satin spar gypsum. Comes out of the bottom of an evaporated seabed from the Permian era, about 250 million years ago."

Salvador's imagination was running wild with the exposure to so much information about Palo Duro Canyon. Excavated remains of giant prehistoric animals and archaic Native American sites. Spanish conquistadors and French explorers. The Comancheros who traded with the Comanches.

And Colonel Mackenzie's battle of Palo Duro Canyon in 1875, just a few miles down the canyon from where they were camping.

Running Eagle's mind was also on fire, but for another reason. "What'd you think of that girl we saw today?"

Salvador smiled. "You talkin' about the ranchers' daughter who couldn't stop staring at you?"

"I can't quit thinking about her either. Not sure why. I've seen lots of pretty girls before. Anyway, I'm pretty sure she wouldn't be interested in me. Got nothing to offer her."

"That's not what her eyes were saying."

Running Eagle smiled. "Yea, she was checking me out pretty hard. Wonder if she'll be at Tascosa's ranch tomorrow night."

"Maybe. Hard to say how a woman thinks. Or what they'll do. Not that I'm an expert or anything. I've only had one girlfriend in my life."

"Only one?"

"Yeah. Remember when I told you about the guy I beat up for attacking my girlfriend? That's her. Samantha. She's probably already got another boyfriend by now. Guys were always checking her out."

"I don't know. Girls think different about that kind of stuff. If they're really interested they'll stick with a guy, even if he's not around. I think it gives them something to talk about with other girls."

Sal nodded. "Yea, you could be right."

Running Eagle stood, picked up a walking stick he'd made from a golf club and pointed in a southeast direction.

"*The Lighthouse Trail* is just a few miles away on the canyon loop. Probably the most popular hike in the canyon, besides the CCC Trail. We'll get up early so we can knock both of them out. See you in the morning."

"Sounds good. I'll pour water on the fire before I crash. Manana."

Salvador sat motionless in the dark of the night, watching the shadows of the fire play among the trees and boulders.

Though only twenty miles from Amarillo, it seemed as if he were in a faraway land. *A stranger to the panhandle, he somehow felt he was at home.*

CHAPTER 74

Tascosa hardly slept Saturday night. He tossed and turned, thinking about the contents of the box rumored to be buried in Rag Town City.

Over the course of his career he'd found some old letters and documents that had led to valuable information. And discoveries.

And with his knowledge of the area, he was convinced that there was a treasure trove of valuable artifacts in the Texas Panhandle waiting to be discovered. Hidden relics of history buried in the ground or stored in the cracks and crevices of old buildings.

It was 11 am on Sunday when Tascosa turned onto Sixth Street looking for a parking spot. Sixth Street. Old Route 66, The Mother Road. In Amarillo it was the heart of the antique district. The place he'd begun his career, developing numerous contacts in the business.

He parked his car in front of the Golden Light Café and entered. In a booth by the front door was the Sixth Street Mall antique dealer, sipping a coke. He looked up when Tascosa walked in.

"Morning Walt. Heard you might be moving over to Nat's Ballroom Antiques. That true?"

"No reason to move. Sixth Street Mall's been the top-rated antique store in Amarillo for almost a decade. But I like Nat's. It's got some good stuff and a lot of music history."

Tascosa took a seat in the booth opposite Walt. "Uncle Zippo said you might have picked up something of interest."

The waitress approached their booth. "Hey Tascosa, Walt already ordered. You want your usual?"

"Please. Make sure you give me the check. Walt bought last time."

Walt waited for the waitress to leave before picking up a shoe box in the seat beside him and placing it on the table.

"Found this stuff in an abandoned house off Amarillo Boulevard, just behind Wildhorse Lake." Walt picked up the papers inside the box and spread them out, looking at Tascosa with a solemn face. "I've read through this stuff several times. Might be the best stash of information I've found in ten years."

Tascosa felt an adrenaline rush as he slowly and methodically worked his way through the old receipts and letters. Finally, he picked up a hand-drawn map and studied it for several minutes before replacing it into the box.

He looked at Walt skeptically. "There's a big 'X' on MAP-C, directly below the site of a saloon-gambling house, 100 feet south of Wildhorse Lake. Says that's where the gold is."

Walt nodded. "Yea, south of the lake between Georgia and Washington. Tascosa, I've heard lots of tales about the Casner Gold. But the only thing I know for sure is that nobody's found it yet. At least no one has claimed to have found it."

Tascosa looked at Walt, trying to act like his normal self. Calm, relaxed, and in control. This box of letters and maps were a rare find, no doubt about it. He hadn't seen or heard of any new information about the lost gold in quite a while.

"Could be something to it. I've been chasin' this story for a long time, and this might be the best information I've come across. What kind of a trade you got in mind for the box of papers?"

Walt's smile started slowly and continued until his entire face lit up like a Christmas tree. There was an antique sitting on a desk at Adobe Ranch he'd tried to pry away from Tascosa for years.

"I think you know what I want."

Tascosa returned a sheepish smile, knowing Walt had the upper hand.

"You want that 1857 Smith and Wesson that I bought at a barn sale outside Mobeetie, owned by the famous Texas gambler: *The CATFISH KID.*"

"Yep. That's the one. Still got it?"

"Sittin' on my desk, same place it was the last time you tried to trade me out of it. Looks like it's gonna have a new home."

Tascosa stood and dropped two twenties on the table.

"I'm having a few people over for dinner tonight at the ranch. Smokin' a brisket. If you don't have plans why don't you come by and join us. After dinner we'll close the deal."

Walt nodded. "Count me in, but I might be a little late. Go ahead and take the box of papers. I'll pick up the gun tonight."

It'd been awhile since Tascosa had been this excited. He told himself to calm down. The information in the box he'd looked at might be another dead-end trail, one of many he'd chased in his career.

He also reminded himself that it had always been the chase for the treasure that excited him, not the actual treasure itself.

And the stories. After all, that's how he'd gotten his name.

CHAPTER 75

Peshlakai's truck was parked next to the silversmith shop at Adobe Ranch when Tascosa pulled in. The sliding door to the Santa Fe train car was wide open and he could hear the grinding of stone. He parked next to the truck and walked into the shop.

Peshlakai stopped, lifted his safety glasses and looked up. "Been awhile since I used this old machine. Still works as good as it did when we installed it twenty-five years ago. Take a look at this stone."

Tascosa took the turquoise cabochon Peshlakai was shaping and lifted it to the light. *"Lavender Pit Bisbee.* High grade. $40 to $50 a carat."

Peshlakai nodded, pushed back from the wooden bench and picked up the silver bolo he'd been working on all morning.

"I made it the same way the old smiths did back in the day: melted old Morgan silver dollars, file and stamp work with handmade tools."

Peshlakai laid the bolo on top of a large antique anvil, set the polished blue stone into the bezel and strapped the bolo around his neck. "What'duya think?"

"You still got the touch. That's the nicest old-school bolo I've seen in years."

Tascosa took the box he was carrying under his arm and placed it on the work bench. "Peshlakai, got a minute? I need you to look at something I just traded for. Something I've been huntin' for decades." Tascosa pulled Map-C out of the box and laid it on the table.

Peshlakai examined the small hand-drawn map of Rag Town and quickly found his eyes fixed on the 'X' by the old saloon.

"The CASNER GOLD?" Peshlakai asked, a sense of anticipation in his voice.

Tascosa nodded. "I think this is the real deal. Let's go to the research office next door and look at the map on the wall. See if we can find the saloon and get an exact location of the box."

They entered a door on the north side of the railroad car, walked past several historic maps of the panhandle, then stopped by a desk in the corner of the room.

"Here it is. A large-scale grid map of Rag Town City. And here's the saloon." Tascosa placed his finger on the map, just south of the saloon. "Gold should be located about right here!"

Peshlakai looked at Tascosa. "How much gold did they bury?"

"$20,000 in gold coins, minted at Carson City Nevada in the 1870's."

Both men turned around at the sound of a vehicle pulling into the ranch. They exited the room, closed the door and walked back to the silversmith shop.

Running Eagle eased his 4-Runner past the Texas and American flags that flanked both sides of the gate. He parked close to the entrance and headed toward the open train car where Tascosa and Peshlakai were standing.

"Tascosa, want us to unload the flea market merchandise back into the storage area?"

"Be much appreciated, if you don't mind."

Running Eagle stopped by the smoker on his way to the van and lifted the lid. "We're starving. What time's dinner?"

"Brisket will be ready in about five minutes. Pot of beans and two skillets of cornbread are on the stone stove."

Sal followed Running Eagle to Tascosa's van. They carried the excess items from the flea market to the storage area inside the Santa Fe train car.

Entering the room on the south side of the silversmith shop, Running Eagle stopped and scanned the four large shelves. Each shelf was six-foot tall and twenty-foot long, bulging with valuable antiques.

"Yogee, we put the paleo bones and archeological finds on Row-1. Row-2 is for antiques during the European period, 1521 to 1875. Row-3 and 4 are for items dated after 1876. Should be an ID tag or sticker on each item."

They walked up and down the rows, placing each item into its designated bin before leaving the room.

As they passed Peshlakai, Salvador examined the scattered tools and machines used to cut and polish stones, and the gas tank with a torch to melt silver into jewelry.

"So, this is a silversmith workbench. How long you been making jewelry Peshlakai?"

"Long time. Started training with my father when I was ten."

Peshlakai picked up the bolo he'd been working on all

morning.

"Sal, a man needs a bolo when he's in the Southwest, so I decided to make you one. Hope you like it. Let's see if it fits." Peshlakai carefully placed the bolo around Sal's neck, making sure the tips lined up.

"It's awesome Peshlakai. First bolo I've ever had. I can't believe you made this for me." Sal stared at the bolo and kept his hand on the stone.

Peshlakai abruptly turned around, startled by the sound of a car speeding down the dirt road that led to the ranch. The car barreled past the gates and pulled up to the stone stove. The drivers' side door flew open and out stepped Uncle Zippo, a serious look on his face. He hurriedly walked toward the train car.

"Evening Tascosa, Peshlakai. *Where's them cornbread and beans Tim's mom made?*"

CHAPTER 76

Texas Tim slowly maneuvered his Tundra into Adobe Ranch and parked it next to the entrance. He grabbed his 5-iron and his driver as he exited the vehicle and walked over to the outdoor oven.

Uncle Zippo looked up just long enough to see who it was, then lowered his head back to the plate of food.

"How's them beans and cornbread Zip?"

Uncle Zippo stopped eating, wiped his mouth on his shirt sleeve and pointed a finger at Tim.

"SON…let me TELL you 'bout yo mama's cookin'. This might be the BEST plate of groceries in the Texas Panhandle. MAYBE the whole STATE!"

"Can't argue with that. Hey, Running Eagle, when you're finished eating, let's walk back to Tascosa's driving range and hit a few. We gotta keep the rust off for that big tournament coming up in a few weeks."

Running Eagle quickly devoured the remainder of his brisket, grabbed his driver out of the 4-Runner and followed Tim.

Tascosa watched the two golfers as they disappeared over a small hill in the distance, then looked over at Sal.

"Yogee, Peshlakai told me you got your place all cleaned up. Said you might need a little more reading material. Let's head over to the house. I've got a few extra books in my library you might find interesting."

Sal followed Tascosa over to the adobe house, stepped up on the porch and walked inside.

Tascosa led Salvador to the open living room where a wooden bookshelf had been built into the wall. Every inch was covered with books. Grabbing a small cardboard box from under the table, Tascosa picked out an eclectic assortment of non-fiction titles and stacked them carefully inside the container.

Darwin's *Voyage of the Beagle*, Scott Peck's *Road Less Traveled*, Shelby Steele's *The Content of Our Character*, Kahlil Gibran's *The Prophet*, Kent Nerburn's *Neither Wolf Nor Dog*, Phil Cousineau's *Art of Pilgrimage*, Carl Sagan's *Cosmos*, and Joseph Campbell's *Power of Myth*.

He also added a few western novels to the box: Hillerman's *Thief of Time*, Zane Grey's *Wonderer of the Wasteland*, and *Shalako* by Louis L'Amour.

"Let's see here, I need to get you one more book. Ah, here it is." Tascosa reached up and pulled down a book that seemed to have special meaning. He handed it to Sal.

"*Maverick Town*, by John McCarty. Written in 1946. One of the best books ever written about the wild-west town of Old Tascosa. Here you go. I've got some extra copies."

Sal flipped quickly through the book, then looked up. "Same as your name, Tascosa."

"Yep. I was raised at Cal Farley's Boy's Ranch, thirty miles south of Amarillo. That's where the city of Old Tascosa use to be. Right there on the banks of the Canadian River. Only a couple of buildings left now, and a few tumbled down ruins."

"That's where you got your name, Old Tascosa?"

Tascosa nodded. "I was seven when my mom sent me there. Soon as I arrived I started hearin' tales about outlaws, gunfights, buried gold and famous people of the west."

"Characters like Billy the Kid, Pat Garrett and Charles Goodnight. I'd walk around Boy's Ranch all day asking anyone I could about Old Tascosa. Pretty soon, every time someone saw me coming they would say, *'Here comes Tascosa.'*"

CHAPTER 77

Salvador, Tascosa and Uncle Zippo were relaxing on the front porch of Adobe Ranch when a large black truck pulled into the yard. A beautiful young woman dressed in a fitted summer skirt stepped out of the truck and walked toward the porch.

"Hi Tascosa, sorry I'm late. Had to drop dad off at the Quarter Horse Association and I got caught in some traffic."

Tascosa walked down the steps of the porch and over to Sierra, his best friend's daughter. He'd known her since she was a little girl.

"Glad you could make it. Come on over and we'll get you a plate of BBQ."

Sierra scanned the yard, feeling a tinge of disappointment. She fidgeted and continued to look, trying to see if he was there. "I'm not real hungry Tascosa, but I would like a glass of tea if you have some."

Tascosa noticed Sierra as she continued to scan the area, apparently on a quest to locate something. Or someone.

Rex had called him earlier in the day and told him that

Sierra had been asking lots of questions about Running Eagle. The type of questions women ask when they're interested in a man.

Tascosa handed Sierra a glass of tea and went back to his chair on the front porch. He grinned when he asked the question. *"Looking for something?"*

Sierra smiled innocently. "Oh, just looking around the place. Hadn't been here in a while. Is anyone else coming to dinner tonight?"

"Not sure, but Texas Tim and Running Eagle are out back on the driving range, trying to stay sharp for a tournament coming up in a few weeks."

Sierra's heart skipped a beat when she heard his name. Running Eagle. She'd thought about him a lot since she first saw him on Saturday. Asked her father a lot of questions. But there were still so many things that she did not know.

"He plays golf?"

"Yep. Started playing with Tim when I took him over there six months ago to do some trading. At first, Tim just helped him with his driver and his irons at the car lot. Next thing you know they were playing 18-holes of golf twice a week. Tim said he had one of the most natural left-handed swings he'd ever seen."

Sierra nodded. "Guess I'll walk back and see how they're doing."

Sierra's heart was beating fast, her mind racing. She walked back to the rustic driving range that Tascosa and her father had created for her when she was fourteen years old. She stopped about twenty feet away and watched.

Running Eagle stepped up to the tee-box with his driver and effortlessly blasted the ball on a straight line to within a few feet of the 300-yard flagpole in the distance.

Tim was standing ten feet away from the tee-box when, from the corner of his eye, he saw someone approach. He turned around and noticed that Sierra had stopped a short distance away, her eyes fixed on Running Eagle as if in a trance.

"What do think Sierra? Think he'll be able to compete?"

Sierra stood there in that moment and heard no sound. Nothing but the avalanche of words that were cascading through her own mind.

Sierra, what's wrong with you?

You're an intelligent, successful, independent women who just graduated with a masters' degree.

So why are you standing out in the middle of a field, staring at an ex-convict who lives in a tent behind the flea market?

CHAPTER 78

Tim pulled into the car lot on Monday morning and looked around. He parked and walked slowly through the lot, closely examining each of the cars. All were clean and in perfect running condition. *This Yogee kid was something.*

He entered the office and scanned the room. Everything was immaculately organized and in place.

Rrrrrriiinnnngggg!!

"Hello, this is Tim…Morning Tascosa, great smoked ribs last night. What?…Yea, we both got lucky hiring this kid. He's honest, works hard, never complains, respectful, and does what needs to be done without being told…What's that?…Noticed that myself. Tradin' seems to come natural to him, like he's been doin' it all his life. I'm 'bout to go tell him the good news. Later."

Tim picked up the coffee that had been freshly brewed and poured himself a cup before walking over to the open front door of the '66 Traveco.

"Morning Yogee, car lot looks great. Tascosa handed me a small packet last night, wanted me to give it to you today.

It's about the sale of your buffalo skull. Come on over and we'll take a look at the numbers."

Sal put down the book he was reading and followed Tim to the office.

Sitting at his desk, Tim opened a manila folder and pulled out a piece of paper. "This is the breakdown of the sale of the buffalo skull that Tascosa brokered with one of his collectors. Take a look at the numbers and see if everything is correct."

Sal pulled a chair up to Tim's desk and looked at the money he'd just gotten for the skull. *SALE PRICE: $12,000.*

"Twenty five percent of the sale is the broker fee Tascosa charges for any deal he executes. Same as Paleo, and the same percentage I charge. Notice that half of the $3,000 broker's fee will go to Running Eagle, since he and Peshlakai brought the skull to Tascosa. It's called a 'bird-dog' fee, or a finder's fee."

Sal looked up from the paper. "So, I get $9,000 for an old sun-bleached buffalo skull I found in the shrubs of a dry riverbed?"

"That's how it works. Tascosa sold the skull for $12,000. The broker fee is $3,000. You get $9,000. Do the numbers look right?"

Salvador looked at Tim, speechless. $9,000. He couldn't believe it.

Texas Tim stood and walked over to the customer PUTT-FOR-THE-GREEN area. He lined up several balls ten feet from the hole and began to practice.

"Yogee, last Thursday you said you needed a vehicle, and that when you got the money, the first thing you would do would be to buy a car. Well, you got enough money now to pay cash for almost any vehicle on my lot."

Sal stood and looked out the window at the cars on the lot.

He'd cleaned and driven every vehicle for the past several days and was very familiar with each one.

"Do I have enough for the silver 2009 Toyota Tacoma?"

Tim stopped putting and walked toward the door. "More than enough. I'm only going to charge you what I paid for it: $5500. Why don't you grab the keys and take it for a test drive while I go talk to one of my long-time customers."

An 18-foot U-Haul had pulled into the lot and parked. The driver's door opened and out stepped a middle-aged man wearing a straw hat, sunglasses, khaki shorts and a white, long sleeved Corona t-shirt.

The man shook Tim's hand before pointing toward the alley behind the back of the car lot. After a few minutes, Tim stuck his head into the front door of the office.

"Yogee, keep an eye on the lot. I gotta step out into the alley and do a little 'dumpster divin'." Both men disappeared around the building.

Sal walked over to a wooden peg board across from Tim's desk, grabbed a set of truck keys and excitedly walked down to the Tacoma. He climbed in and looked around a few minutes before turning the ignition switch.

RRRMMMM! Started easily, smoothly. Just like it had every morning last week. He looked down at the odometer. 122,000 miles.

Gunz told him it was probably the best car on the lot. And even though there were dark oil stains in the carpet, ripped seats and dents all over the body, he assured him that this vehicle would easily go 300,000 miles with regular maintenance.

Sal turned on the radio, rolled down the windows and placed his hands on the steering wheel. Panhandle winds swept across his body, stirring a restlessness that was growing by the day.

He looked out of the front window toward the western horizon, watching a few white clouds float across the sky.

His mind drifted outside the confines of the cab of the truck, and he dreamed of travel west. To a place where he could feel the sun on his face and the wind in his hair. A land where he could be free.

For the first time since he'd left his home in Dallas, Salvador felt he could relax. He had friends, his own place, a full-time job at the car lot, and a part-time job at the flea market.

And by the end of the day, he'd own his own truck and have the freedom to travel.

CHAPTER 79

The elevator stopped at the 2nd floor of the Dallas County Courthouse. Officer Perrez exited, took a left down the hallway and entered Judge Atkenz chambers.

"Morning officer", the secretary smiled. "The judge is expecting you. Can I get you something to drink?"

"Won't be necessary," he replied abruptly. "Don't plan to stay long." He walked to the first door on the right and entered the judge's office.

The judge looked up. "Mr. Perrez, I'm looking over the list of cases I've got coming up next week, and that Salvador Gonzalez kid you arrested for felony assault is crossed off. Now, you can correct me if I'm wrong, but didn't he almost beat a man to death?"

Officer Perrez grimaced. "Put him in the hospital, critical condition."

"I thought you said we had that case wrapped up? There's been a lot of press on that story, and I was countin' on puttin' that kid away for about 25 years."

Perrez took a chair in front of a massive walnut desk. "I

thought we had him, since his bail was set at $100,000. But someone walked in and paid it, then the kid skipped town."

Judge Atkenz pushed his chair back. "Not tryin' to take over your job, but I just want to remind you that my election's coming up, and our supporters have already invested over $125,000 in my re-election. We need to get as many convictions as we can and every case counts. Includin' this one."

Officer Perrez nodded. "I've put a few of my best detectives on the case, one's we can trust. Also got a free-lance journalist on his tail. We've located him in Fort Worth, where he bought a bus ticket to Wichita Falls. He won't get far."

Judge Atkenz reached into his bottom drawer, pulled out an envelope and slid it over to the officer. "Our supporters came by this morning and dropped this off. They want you to know that they appreciate all your hard work."

A measured smile broke out on Officer Perrez's face. He opened the envelop and thumbed through the money before stuffing it into his pocket.

PART EIGHT

ROADSIDE RELICS

THREE WEEKS LATER...

CHAPTER 80

The sun was rising in the east behind him as he set the cruise control on his Tacoma to 75 mph. He passed the Amarillo city limit sign on I-40 west and continued another ten miles till he reached his destination. *Cadillac Ranch.*

Salvador wanted to get there before the tourists. Wanted to be there early on Friday, his only day off, and see the cars against the backdrop of the morning light.

People at the flea market had been talking about these buried cars and he'd become curious. Wanted to see them for himself.

It was hard to believe that he had been in Amarillo for only four weeks. Seemed much longer. He had mastered the opening of the car lot and felt competent with his basic knowledge of antiques at the flea market.

Exiting off the highway, Sal drove under the overpass and slowly turned onto the I-40 East access road toward the gate entrance.

Success. He was the first one there.

The ten antique Cadillacs sat majestically out in a cow

pasture, buried there by an eccentric millionaire. They were spray painted with every color in the rainbow, tagged with slogans and names of people traveling on the highway.

ROAD ART, they called it, and people traveled from almost every country in the world to see this unique creation.

Spray painting the Cadillacs was an activity that visitors from around the world had been participating in for decades. It was the final ritual that marked the completion of their pilgrimage to this famous roadside attraction.

Caught up in the moment, Sal had himself decided to mark his visit in the same way, so he walked over to a set of dumpsters just past the entrance. He reached down and searched for a few half-empty cans to spray his road name on the Cadillacs.

In the process of his search something caught his eye. It lay toward the back of the dumpster, on top of several used paint canisters.

Salvador casually reached back and picked it up. It was a square, black leather billfold. He opened the wallet and thumbed through the contents. Four credit cards. A young male driver's license with an Amarillo address. A college ID from a local university. And a wad of cash thick enough to choke a mule.

Suddenly, unexpectantly, the shrill sound of a police siren pierced the tranquility of the morning. Sal dropped the billfold and spun around, watching the flashing red lights disappear into the distance.

Sal picked up the billfold and nervously looked around. *There was a lot of money in this wallet, and he'd had enough trouble with the police. He needed to get rid of it, quick! The Cadillacs could wait for another day.* He walked over to his truck, climbed in and headed eastbound on I-40.

Within ten minutes Sal entered the back of the T-Anchor Flea Market, parked on the side of the dirt road off the interstate, and walked out into an open field.

He continued until he came to a big sign on the banks of a playa lake. T-ANCHOR FLEA MARKET. Underneath the sign was his friend and co-worker, lobbing golf balls toward three small flags in the distance, just west of the Cracker Barrel Restaurant.

CHAPTER 81

Running Eagle looked out across the playa lake and located the one-hundred-yard marker. He strategically gripped his sand wedge and stepped up to the golf ball that lay on a four-foot grass turf, just under the T-ANCHOR FLEA MARKET sign.

Slowly, he maneuvered the head of the club inches away from the ball while he positioned his stance. One more look at the yard marker, one more adjustment of his grip and his stance.

Finally, he moved the club backward to the top of the arc before powering it down into the golf ball, lofting the white sphere high into the air. The ball dropped to within a foot of the marker.

"You make it look easy, like you've been playing for twenty years instead of six months."

Running Eagle turned around and smiled at Sal.

"WEST TEXAS OPEN starts tomorrow morning. First tournament I've ever played in, and I'm a little nervous. Tim told me to relax and have fun. Play one shot at a time."

"Guess you won't be working the flea market this weekend."

"Neither are you. Tascosa said he's not setting up. Said you and him would be hanging out at the tournament."

"Heard you and Sierra been hangin' out since the dinner at Tascosa's a few weeks ago."

Running Eagle grinned sheepishly. "Yea. She came over to me and we started talking about golf. Next thing you know it got dark, the stars came out and we built a fire. She gave me her number before she left."

Sal nodded and grinned. "So, you like her?"

"Yea, she's pretty cool. We talk on the phone almost every day. Had a few dates."

"Sounds like you guys are getting' serious."

"I don't know. I think she's gonna take that big job down in Austin, so I need to stay focused on work. And on the tournament tomorrow. How's your day off going?"

Sal moved close to Running Eagle, looked around, and motioned for him to walk behind a small stand of trees twenty feet away.

Once they arrived, Sal looked around again. He pulled the black leather wallet he'd found at Cadillac Ranch out of his backpack and handed it to Running Eagle.

"Take a look at this."

Running Eagle opened the wallet and examined the contents. "Whoa! Look at all that cash. Where'd you get this?"

"Found it this morning by a dumpster at Cadillac Ranch. I felt nervous hangin' onto it, so I drove over here to see what you think I should do."

Running Eagle pulled out the drivers' license and closely examined the picture and the address.

"Looks like a local college kid dropped it. Address is in the

Amarillo area. I'll call Tascosa, see what he has to say."

Running Eagle pulled out his phone and called Tascosa's number. "Tascosa, Running Eagle. Good time or bad time?"

"Good time. Just hangin' out at the coffee shop, working on a few deals. How's practice going?"

"Good, but somethings come up. Yogee's here with me. He found a billfold out by one of the dumpsters at Cadillac Ranch, filled with cash and credit cards. Got a local address on the driver's license."

"Can you read the front side of the license to me?"

Running Eagle slowly read the name and the address of the drivers' license.

Tascosa paused several seconds before responding. "I'm sitting outside on the patio at Starbucks, I-40 and Grand, right next to the drive-thru. Think you could drop the billfold off with me this morning?"

CHAPTER 82

Tascosa sat out on the Starbucks patio and thumbed through the contents of the billfold that Running Eagle had just dropped off. He knew the owner. It was the grandson of a friend he'd done business with for three decades, Judd Masterson.

Judd was a prominent oil man in the Texas Panhandle whom he'd met in the early 1980's, just weeks after Tascosa had quit working as an antique dealer on Sixth Street and struck out on his own.

At that time, Judd was a destitute farmer and rancher who owned nothing but fifty acres of land with poor soil. And a beat-up work truck. Both were heavily financed by the bank.

Judd was so broke he'd begun selling off his family's rare heirloom antiques at the flea market to Tascosa, the only dealer in Amarillo who offered him a fair wholesale price.

Judd's bad luck changed overnight when a local oil wildcatter found a small pocket of high-grade petroleum on his land. He sold all but ten acres for a fair sum of money and gave up his career in farming and ranching. Judd was now a

Texas oilman.

Tascosa double-checked the contents of the billfold, careful to examine every item inside. Finally, he pulled the driver's license out and called his old friend.

"Morning Judd, this is Tascosa. Been a few days since we talked. How in the heck are you?"

"Considering where I was when you first met me, I'd say I've been a lucky man. The oil bidness has treated me a lot better than farmin' and ranchin'. What's on your mind?"

"One of my workers was at Cadillac Ranch this morning, looking at them buried cars out in the field. He found a billfold by one of the dumpsters, and I think it belongs to your grandson. Got it right here with me. There's four credit cards in the wallet and about three thousand in cash."

Tascosa read Judd the name that was on the driver's license, followed by the address. There was several seconds of silence on the other end of the phone, followed by an explosion.

"That Son-Of-A-Bitch! He's been spoiled rotten by my daughter and her husband. Ain't worked a day in his life. Don't get me wrong Tascosa, I love my grandson. But he's caused me a lot of grief through the years."

Tascosa chuckled. "Aw, don't be so hard on him Judd. He'll come around."

"You might be right. And to be honest, I've been a little easy on him myself, him being my only grandson and all. I'm just glad that kid that works for you is honest. How about I buy you lunch today so's I can take a good look at that billfold?"

Tascosa was already inside the steak house when Judd walked up to the table, wearing the same clothes he always wore. Weathered black Justin boots, worn faded wranglers and a pearl-button long sleeved shirt. A sweat-stained Stetson was pulled down halfway on the crown of his head.

The waitress arrived as Judd took his seat in the booth.

"Howdy Judd. Here's your Coors Light. Special today is the combination plate with brisket, sausage, beans and potato salad."

"That'll work just fine Jan, and don't even think about giving the ticket to Tascosa."

Judd picked up the mug and took a long pull on the ice-cold brew. "Ahhhh! My mouth was dry as a bone. Now, let's take a look at that billfold."

Tascosa pulled out the wallet and handed it to Judd. He quickly thumbed through the contents.

Judd made eye contact with Tascosa, a contemplative look on his face.

"Stopped by the bank on my way over here. Banker told me that my grandson had four credit cards that I'd co-signed for, and every one of them sumbitches is maxed out. $60,000 of debt."

Judd took another long drink of his beer, emptying the glass. He looked around the restaurant, seemingly with a loss for words.

"While I was at it, I went ahead and called his mom. Asked her how he's doing in college. She 'hem-hawed' around a minute, then decided to come clean. Said he's run up his student loans to $45,000, and he ain't even halfway through his second year. She'd also received a letter a week ago stating that he's on academic probation because he's failing all his classes. Don't sound like he's learnin' a DAMN thing!"

Judd fiddled with his empty glass of beer, pondering his situation.

"Tascosa, I been thinking. My daughter, and now my

grandson, ain't got no respect for money. Most of that's my fault. I always gave em what they wanted. They never had to work for it. So I decided on my way over here that things got to change, but I ain't sure what to do."

Tascosa nodded. "Yea, sounds like you got a tough decision to make."

"You know he's only 19 years old, and between the credit cards and the school loans he's already over $100,000 in debt. What do you think I should do?"

Tascosa looked back at Judd. "It's not an easy decision to make, but I never tell a man what to do with his family. Particular when it's a good friend like you. I don't want none of the blame if my advice don't work out."

Judd nodded. "I can appreciate that. It's just that I hadn't made a lot of good decisions when it comes to my daughters' family and money. So let me ask you this. If this was YOUR daughter and grandson, what do you think you would do?"

Tascosa took a sip of his ice-tea, hesitant to get involved in family matters. He decided to give the question back to Judd.

"What's your gut feeling tellin' you Judd?"

Judd looked around the restaurant, then down at his empty glass.

"I think I need to pay off the balances on them four credit cards I co-signed for. Then I need to cut 'em up, close the accounts and never sign for another credit card. Let my daughter and my grandson learn about money the hard way, like I did."

Tascosa raised his glass of tea into the air. "That's a damn good plan Judd. Now you're thinking like the good businessman I've known for all these years. Here's to learnin' the hard way."

"And," Judd continued, "I'm a gonna give that boy of yurn

who turned in the billfold an 'Old Judd Thank You'. What'd you say his name was?"

"Yogee. But I can tell you now he ain't looking for no reward."

Judd smiled. "That's exactly why Ole Judd's gonna say thank you to this boy, Mr. Yogee."

CHAPTER 83

Scott sat in the back of the What-A-Burger restaurant in Wichita Falls. He looked out the window, watching the cars pass by on state highway 287.

He had been on a roll with the investigation. A big roll.

The first break came from a detective at the police department who had been assigned to find and monitor Salvador's whereabouts. This detective gave Scott his business card and offered him a small amount of cash if Scott came up with information that could be used for Sal's arrest.

His second break came at the bus station in Fort Worth. A homeless man had recognized the picture of Sal that he had distributed among the drifters hanging out at the station.

The drifter said he'd seen him ride up, leave his bike leaning against the station, and walk in to get a ticket.

Next, he talked to the ticket clerk who had sold Sal his bus ticket. *'Yes, I remember him. Seemed pretty nervous when he got on the bus.'*

That revelation led him to talk to the driver of the bus.

'Yep, I recognize him. He rode the bus to Wichita Falls, but never

reboarded for Amarillo. I specifically remember waiting an extra ten minutes, but he never showed up.'

His fifth clue came from a Wichita Falls security guard at the bus station. Salvador had asked her for directions to What-A-Burger, just off highway 287.

But now here he was at the What-A-Burger in Wichita Falls, and the investigation had completely dried up. He was unable to find a single person who recognized Salvador's picture.

Scott sat speechless. He felt like the wind had been knocked out of him. This was not how the investigation was supposed to end. Salvador was gone. Vanished. And not a trace left behind.

For several weeks he'd been obsessed with finding this kid. He'd spent a lot of time and a lot of money. His checking account had dwindled to microscopic proportions.

Out of leads and out of money, Scott would have to fold up the tent and move on. Salvador Jesus Gonzalez was out there, but he'd failed in his quest to find him.

The somberness of the moment was interrupted by the vibration of his phone. He wondered if that was his mom texting, trying to get him to come back home. Or his ex-girlfriend.

Slowly, he picked up the phone and looked at the number on the screen. He wasn't sure who it was. After a few seconds, he decided to look at the text.

Scott...this is Brendon, sportswriter in Fort Worth...we met four weeks ago... Starbucks on 7th...I THINK I FOUND YOUR MAN!

CHAPTER 84

It was the first day of the West Texas Open and Brendon Holloway had arrived early to cover the tournament. This was an assignment he'd asked for, an assignment where he could work on two stories in one weekend.

First, he wanted to find out more information about Leroy, the homeless vet who'd rescued a dog from the mouth of an alligator. He was certain Leroy had been a star running back in a small town in the Panhandle, and it was rumored that the Dallas Cowboys had offered him a tryout with the team.

Second, he wanted to see for himself the legendary senior golfer from the panhandle, Texas Tim. Document his powerful drives off the tee-box, rumored to be 350 yards long.

The West Texas Open Golf Tournament started slowly, but the competitive positioning was beginning to take shape. After the 5th hole, Texas Tim and his partner Running Eagle were in a three-way tie for first place.

Brendon had followed the golfing duo since the beginning of the tournament, documenting powerful drive after powerful drive. 320 yards, 340 yards, 332 yards, 346 yards, and a remarkable 357 yards. Tim was putting on a show.

But the most surprising part of the tournament was the play of his young partner, Running Eagle. He'd never seen a more fluid left-handed swing, or a golfer more accurate with his irons. Who was this young phenom?

Hole #6 brought the duo back down to earth with a triple bogey, but not for long. They scored an eagle on hole #7, claiming sole possession of first place.

Brendon stopped his cart, put down his notebook and picked up his 35mm Canon Rebel. Attaching the zoom lens into place, he began to take pictures of this dynamic duo. This was the type of story he lived for.

As Brendon was capturing the two golfers on film, three fans who'd been close by walked into the scene. Brendon continued to take pictures.

The first fan was a small, older man who appeared to be in his late 50's, early 60's. He walked up to Tim, smiled, and slapped him on the back.

The second fan was a pretty young woman, about 5'5" tall, wearing golf shorts and a sun visor. She walked directly up to Running Eagle and gently kissed him on the cheek. Must be his wife, or his girlfriend.

Finally, the third fan walked up to the golf cart and shook hands with Running Eagle. He was wearing a Texas Longhorn cap. Brendon lowered his camera and stared at the young man who had just shook hands with Running Eagle.

No, it couldn't be! He quickly picked up his camera and focused the lens on the guy with the Longhorn cap.

Snap!Snap!Snap!Snap!

Brendan put down his camera and picked up his iPhone. Snap!Snap!Snap!Snap! *That's him!* That was the guy with Leroy four weeks ago on the Trinity River. The kid that Scott was looking for but had not yet found.

He quickly searched through his phone until he found the name SCOTT. Logging in the name, he attached the pictures he'd just taken and sent them to the itinerant journalist, along with a brief message.

Scott…this is Brendon, sportswriter in Fort Worth…we met four weeks ago…Starbucks on 7th…I THINK I FOUND YOUR MAN!

CHAPTER 85

There was only one space left at the RV Park off highway 287 when Scott arrived in Amarillo on Sunday afternoon. It was a space closest to the access road with an unobstructed view of Texas Tim's Autos.

Thanks to the tip from Brendon, Scott's investigation was back in business.

Monday morning came quickly, and Scott had strategically situated his car to provide a clear view of the lot.

At 5 am the lights came on in the old RV. Scott got out his binoculars and watched as Salvador went through his morning ritual. Shower. Coffee on. Keys on the wooden peg. Cars all started, and the lot area cleaned.

By 8 am the sun was high enough to provide plenty of light for pictures, and Scott took a variety of action shots that might be useful to the police department.

Snap!Snap!Snap!Snap! Salvador cleaning a Toyota Tacoma. Salvador reading in a lounge chair next to the shell of an old Chevy. Salvador eating breakfast. Salvador displaying cars on the outside of the fence.

Texas Tim rolled into the car lot at 9 am, filled his coffee mug and strolled out to the makeshift tee-box on the outside of the fence.

Scott had taken plenty of pictures, so he moved to the next phase of his investigation: on-site data collection. He jumped into his car and drove over to the car lot.

Salvador approached Scotts' car. "Morning. Looks like it's gonna be a nice day. How can we help you?"

Scott got out of his car and walked up to Sal. "Morning. I'm looking for a used truck. Heard you might have a few."

Sal reached out his hand to Scott. "Name's Yogee, and I do believe we may have a few trucks for you to look at."

Scott feigned interest in two or three of the trucks on the lot and the sales pitch began. Talk about the truck. Test drive. Price. Look at another truck. Test drive. Price. Possible financing options.

And during the test drives and the discussions about each of the vehicles, Scott was able to slowly piece together a profile of sorts about Salvador. Get a sense about what type of person he was. What his interests were. And if he were indeed the dangerous felon that the police department had claimed he was.

After two hours of test drives and discussions about purchasing a vehicle, Salvador threw Scott a curve ball.

"Tim always makes burgers on Monday. Want some lunch?"

Scott responded without thinking. "Sure. I was starting to get hungry." Within minutes Scott and Salvador were sitting inside the '66 Traveco at his kitchen table, eating a grilled cheeseburger.

Scott looked around. Books on the table, books on the kitchen counter, books on the dashboard close to the steering wheel. Looks like he had a veracious appetite for information.

"How do you like RV living?"

"Love it. Feel like I'm on the road. Hope to be doing that real soon. Traveling through the southwest, then the rest of the country. Like to go to Europe too, and maybe the Middle East."

"Yea, love traveling myself. Wouldn't mind having a small RV to haul around the country and explore. Stop when I find something interesting."

After an hour or so Scott caught himself relaxing. Enjoying the talk of travel. And of history and antiques and automobiles. He found that he really liked this young man who had been identified as a felon by the police department.

And from out of nowhere an inconvenient thought entered Scott's mind. He tried to ignore it.

"Thanks for the lunch Yogee. I'll think about which of the trucks I like and get back to you."

Scott exited Texas Tim's with a full-blown war raging inside his mind. Most of the chaos came from the information he'd uncovered at a meeting with the detective at the police department three weeks ago.

He'd spent several hours talking with the detective, getting information about the felony that Salvador had committed. But most of the answers to his questions didn't make sense.

He'd also met with teachers and students at Salvador's high school. Talked briefly with his girlfriend Samantha. Even had breakfast at the Waffle House where Salvador's mom worked.

He had the feeling that something wasn't right. That Salvador might not have committed the felony he was charged with. Instead, Salvador may have simply caught a man attempting to rape his girlfriend and tried to save her life.

282

Maybe Sal overreacted, but Sal's actions did not sound like he was a criminal who'd committed a felony. An editorial in the local newspaper flatly stated that the charge was bogus. Maybe even politically motivated.

Had his desire for some under-the-table cash from the detective clouded his judgement?

Scott drove into his space at the RV Park and cut off his car. He reached into the glove box and pulled out a small leather folder where he'd placed the business card of the police detective in charge of the investigation.

Opening the leather folder, he pulled out the card of the man he'd met a few weeks earlier and stared at the name on the front.

He had only to dial the number, tell him the location of Salvador Jesus Gonzalez, and the police could move in for an arrest.

PART NINE

CALL OF THE EAGLE

5 MONTHS LATER...

CHAPTER 86

Salvador took a slow sip of coffee and looked out the window at the dark grey clouds rolling in. Temperatures had plummeted into the 20's over the past few hours, ushering in a cold November blue norther.

But inside his RV it was warm. The small space heater provided a cozy atmosphere for his twenty-seven-foot mobile living space.

Six months had passed since he'd first arrived in Amarillo and Sal had stayed busy, working twelve hours a day, six to seven days a week.

In addition, Tim had given him almost complete control of managing the car lot, as Gunz had been spending more time in Houston. Sal had become Tim's right-hand man, mastering all aspects of the business.

Among the antique dealers in the Texas Panhandle and on Sixth Street, he was becoming known as a savvy trader, respected for both his impeccable honesty and his ability to close a deal.

His skill at buying and selling had allowed him to

accumulate an inventory of over 1,000 antique and collectable items for the market, enough to go into business for himself.

He also owned the 1966 Dodge Traveco RV, which was now updated, remodeled, and furnished. Along with two-acres of prime real estate in north Amarillo, just two miles from Adobe Ranch. And of course, the 2009 Toyota Tacoma.

And no debt.

Sal reached down and picked up his coffee, steam rising from the smoky brew. Slowly, he lifted the cup to his...

BAM!! BAM!! BAM!! "SALVADOR JESUS GONZALEZ! OPEN UP...I KNOW YOU'RE IN THERE."

Sal's hand jerked, spilling the coffee across the table and onto his clothes. He jumped as the hot liquid penetrated his jeans and burnt the flesh on his legs.

Had the police finally caught up with him?

After all these months living off the grid, had they somehow located his hideout? And just as he was thinking about drifting west.

Frantically he looked around for an escape route, but there was none to be found. He'd replayed his arrest scene over in his mind many times, and it always ended the same way. *Hand cuffs. Hauled away in a police car. Thrown into jail for twenty-five years.*

But he'd decided from day one that if they found him, he was not going to fight the police and risk getting injured. Or killed. He would accept his fate, whatever it was.

Reluctantly, Sal walked over to his front door and opened it. A strong north wind pierced the warmth of his trailer.

Standing just inches from the entrance was an athletically built man wearing a leather jacket and a motorcycle helmet. Without asking permission the man pushed through the doorway and sat down on one of the small chairs in his living area.

Sal watched with a sense of uncertainty as the man took off his helmet, revealing long brown uncombed hair. He sat the helmet on top of the bookshelf and with penetrating blue eyes stared at the young man before him.

"I never got that last homework assignment you were supposed to turn in. Remember? A summary of the 1972 movie 'Kung Fu' with David Carradine?"

CHAPTER 87

Mr. T removed his black leather riding gloves and extended his hand toward Sal. "Been a few days Salvador. Looks like you've stayed hidden from the long arm of the law."

Salvador froze momentarily in disbelief, followed by an overwhelming sense of relief and joy at the sight his favorite teacher. A smile broke out across his face. He grabbed his teachers' hand and gripped it tightly, tears welling up in his eyes.

"Mr. T...how'd you find me?"

"Kept my ear close to the ground. Got a few tips from Peshlakai. Then Paleo contacted me and told me that you were working for one of his old golfing buddies, Texas Tim."

"Paleo knows Texas Tim?"

"They've played a few rounds together."

"How come you're not in school, teaching?"

Mr. T smiled. "Guess you lost track of time since you've been drifting. It's Thanksgiving break, so I took a few extra days off to take a road trip. Needed to get out of Dallas. Find a former student of mine and give him some good news. You haven't heard?"

Sal's face was blank. "Heard what?"

"I've brought something from Dallas to deliver to you. Something you might be interested in."

Mr. T stood, took off his backpack and dropped it on the kitchen table. Unzipping the big compartment, he pulled out several letters and a big manila envelope.

Sal walked over to the kitchen cupboard. He pulled down a cup, filled it with hot coffee, and sat it down by Mr. T. "Hope you like it. Dark roast from Indonesia."

Mr. T picked up the cup and took a few sips. "Well now, I guess I did teach you something before you left town."

Salvador stared at the three letters on the table. They were labeled with familiar names: Mom. Samantha. Zane. He stacked them on the corner of the table. He'd read them later when he was alone.

Nervously, Sal picked up the big manila folder with a professional stamp embedded on the opening flap: CONFIDENTIAL FILE FROM THE POLICE DEPARTMENT: SALAVADOR JESUS GONZALEZ. He looked over at Mr. T.

"Go ahead. Open it."

Salvador's fingers shook as he opened the top of the manila folder and pulled out the single sheet of paper inside. He recognized it as a copy of the official letter he'd signed agreeing to the court date he'd skipped when he left Dallas seven months ago.

In large, bold black letters the police department had stamped the words: *CASE DISMISSED. OCTOBER 30th*.

CHAPTER 88

Brendon opened the door to the Starbucks off Mockingbird in Dallas and entered, leaving behind the frigid winds from the north. Looking around, he spotted a counter seat by the front window and headed that way.

After placing his notebook on the wooden bar next to his chair, he walked up to the barista.

"Good morning sir, how can I help you?"

"Grande dark with room, blueberry muffin, and the Dallas paper."

The barista nodded. "Here's your coffee. The muffin will be ready in a few minutes."

Brendon grabbed his coffee and the newspaper before heading back to his seat. Once there, he eased up on the barstool, tossed the newspaper on the counter and opened it up to the local Metro section.

At the top of the page was the headline he was looking for. LOCAL HIGH SCHOOL STUDENT EXONERATED. A smile opened broadly across his face when he read the name of the author of the story.

Just before he finished reading the article, there was a tap on the outside window in front of him. A young man layered in winter garb waved at Brendon, then entered the café.

"Morning Mr. Holloway. Be right there." Scott picked up his coffee and walked toward the veteran sportswriter, hanging his coat on the back of the chair.

"Scott, this is one hell of a story. How did you piece it all together?"

Scott beamed at the compliment. "A little shoe leather, and a lot of luck."

Brendon smiled and shook his head. "What I'm curious about is when did you know Salvador Gonzalez was innocent, since you told me in Amarillo you were about to turn him in to the cops?"

Scott took a sip of the hot brew and looked out the window. "You know, when I interviewed the detective in May, a lot of his answers to my questions didn't make sense. So, I decided to talk with people who knew Sal. His mom, his teachers, his friends, and his girlfriend. I pretty much knew something wasn't right after that."

Scott sat his coffee down and placed his hands on the long wooden bar. "I almost made a big mistake in Amarillo, till I went over to the car lot where Sal was working and got to know him. That's when I decided to go back to Dallas. Find out what really happened, and why he got charged."

"Wait a minute. How did you get all those details about phone calls between the judge and the detective? AND, that Pensacola police arrest report on James Benson?"

"Pure luck. I walked out to my car one morning, and there was a packet in the front seat, no writing, no nothing. Have no idea who dropped it off. I opened it up, and there were two pieces of papers. One, a copy of an official phone conversation between the detective and the judge. The other, a copy of Benson's arrest in Florida. I followed up, and bingo."

Brendon nodded and smiled. "You know, it may be more than beginners' luck. The only two articles you've ever written have been featured in major market newspapers. Ever thought about a career in journalism?"

Scott smiled. "Started another article a month ago. About a homeless guy in Dallas who lives under the bridge. Makes a living selling antiques and dinosaur bones. Goes by the name of Paleo."

Brendon smiled. "Sounds like you're hooked."

Scott looked over at Brendon. "By the way, whatever happened to that article you were writing about Leroy being recruited by the Dallas Cowboys?"

CHAPTER 89

The sun dropped below the rim of Palo Duro Canyon, leaving a yellow-orange glow on the western horizon.

This was the third and final night of his camping trip, and he'd had plenty of quiet time to read. Time to think, and time to digest his new reality. Salvador was a free man. His life as a fugitive of the law had come to an end.

He'd been on the run for six months, hiding from the police. Always on edge. Wondering when they would show up in the middle of the night and take him away in handcuffs.

Surely it would be an easy decision now to travel back to Dallas and pick up his life where he'd left it. Move back in with his mom. Finish high school. Hang out with Zane. And reconnect with Samantha, the only girl he'd ever cared about.

But six months on the road had changed him. He was not the same person he was when he climbed on his bike in early May and rode down to the Trinity River, leaving behind the only life he'd ever known.

The truth was he loved the freedom of being on his own, and the action of the marketplace.

And there was something else. A feeling, an idea that had eased into his body after months of looking into the big Texas sky from the front seat of his RV. *A stirring, a restlessness. It was a call to travel west.*

He'd talked with Tascosa, Tim, and Running Eagle about his situation. Showed them the letter from the police department. Told them about his desire to drift west. They all told him the same thing. Be patient. No need to rush a decision. Weigh the positives against the negatives.

Tascosa suggested he go down into Palo Duro Canyon, camp out for a few days. Read, hike, journal. The right decision would come.

Salvador picked up a stick and stirred the coals in the fire of his campsite. Flames jumped into the coolness of the November night, causing a warmth to creep over his body.

The three letters delivered by Mr. T lay on a rock close by the fire. He'd read through them several times.

Zane was at the University of Texas, majoring in Astronomy. He'd be spending the summer living and working at the McDonald Observatory just north of Alpine, Texas.

Samantha was living at home, finishing her basics at the community college, working with her mom on the weekends at the Canton Flea Market. Hoping Salvador would come home soon.

And then there was the letter from his mom.

Salvador. I miss you more than you can ever know. Please forgive me for my shortcomings as a mother. I wish I could go back and change some things, but I can't. Just to know that you're still alive and well brings happiness back to my life. And now that your case has been dismissed, I look forward to seeing you soon. Please forgive me. I miss you. I love you. Mom.

Sal was torn. He longed to see his mom. He needed to see

his mom.

But there was another equally powerful force inside, pulling him to the openness of the southwest. He found himself unable to control the feeling. The road called him night and day, creating a restlessness he'd never experienced.

He paced anxiously around the campfire, rolling his dilemma over and over in his mind till his body begged for sleep. Finally, he drenched the fire with water, climbed into his tent, and fell into a restless sleep.

CHAPTER 90

Salvador reached into the access cab of his truck and maneuvered the suitcase into place beside his camping gear.

Next, he placed a beat-up guitar Texas Tim found dumpster diving, on the floorboard of the cab. Sal had already learned a few songs. Maybe he'd have time to learn a few more. Besides, Tim said an old guitar is good company on the road, whether you play it or not.

The flashlight was situated in the glove box. His backpack, stuffed with books and journals, on the front seat beside him. Hot coffee in the drink holder below the gearshift. Suitcase in the back.

Tim walked slowly up to the drivers' side of the truck, a seven iron in his left hand. He smiled as he looked inside at the suitcase and the guitar and the backpack.

"The drifters trail. Always something magic about heading west. No agenda, no plan. Just get in your car and roll down the highway."

Salvador smiled and reached his hand out to Tim. "Thanks for understanding Tim. Tell Tascosa and Running

297

Eagle I'll be back in about a week or two unless I decide to keep traveling. Hope mom understands. And Samantha."

Tim nodded. "Not sure if a woman can understand a man's need to drift. Every man has to follow his own path. Anyway, we'll hold the fort down while you're gone, and I'll transfer the two acres Judd Masterson gifted you into your name. Your real name."

"Hard to believe Judd gave me those two acres in North Amarillo just for turning in a lost billfold."

"Sal, you've got to realize that when you turned in that billfold, you forced Judd to look at his relationship with his grandson. And his daughter. He said it was the best thing that's happened to him in decades. Trust me, Judd ain't hurtin' for money."

Tim lifted his seven iron and tapped the bed of Sal's truck.

"Now, get this junk off my lot and get on down the road. Take as much time as you need. I'll see you when you get back."

Sal looked over at his 1966 RV, a feeling of melancholy overtaking him. He'd spent the past six months living inside the vintage mobile vehicle. It had become his home, his first home.

Reluctantly he started the truck and exited the car lot. Jumped on highway 287 North, exited at Loop 335 and headed west till he reached I-40 at Saucy. Finally, he was at the entrance to a road he'd thought about for months. Even dreamed about. Interstate 40 West.

Salvador turned right and eased his truck onto the highway. He passed the Amarillo city limit sign, Cadillac Ranch, and the small community of Wilderado. *And then the sky opened up, pulling his vehicle into the vortex.* He set the cruise control at 75 mph and floated west toward the vast unknown.

THE END.